A Killer Coffee Mystery

Book Four

BY
TONYA KAPPES

TONYA KAPPES
WEEKLY NEWSLETTER

Want a behind-the-scenes journey of me as a writer?
The ups and downs, new deals, book sales, giveaways and more? I share it all! Join the exclusive Southern Sleuths private group today! Go to www.patreon.com/Tonyakappesbooks

As a special thank you for joining, you'll get an exclusive copy of my cross-over short story, *A CHARMING BLEND.* Go to Tonyakappes.com and click on subscribe at the top of the home page.

CHAPTER ONE

The blinding dazzle of the sunrise path on Lake Honey Springs was breathtaking from the Bean Hive Coffeehouse's front windows. The rainbow sheen of oil left on the water from a passing boater was a sure sign that summer was near.

Every time I walked past the front windows of my coffeehouse, I took the time to stop, peer out, and take in the beauty that made living in Honey Springs, Kentucky so inviting.

Debbie Cane, my soon to be sister-in-law, walked up behind me and looked over my shoulder, holding a ceramic coffee mug that had the Bean Hive Coffeehouse logo on it. "I swear you've got the best spot on Honey Lake Boardwalk. And the best coffee." She stuck her nose in the steam of the warm summer blend.

Wait for it, I thought as I watched her close her eyes, her chest lifting with her inhale and a smile curving along her perfectly hot-pink-painted lips.

There it is, I thought, sighing with a feeling of joy bubbling up in my heart. That expression alone was the reason I left my job as a lawyer, moved to Honey Springs, and opened a coffeehouse.

Okay, to be honest—because I always felt like I was in a courtroom under oath and really never had a great poker face—I moved to Honey

Springs because I'd found my law partner, who was also my husband at the time, doing more than client consulting. Maybe it was consulting, but not in the typical way. All of *my* consulting with clients was with clothes on. Regardless, it wasn't my idea of a partnership, professionally or personally.

I licked my wounds and found myself lost in many coffee shops until I realized one day that I too wanted to own a small coffee shop.

"I'm glad you like it." I patted Debbie on the arm.

"I need a favor." She clamped her teeth together with her mouth open a little and a look of hope in her eyes. Her amber hair hung past her earlobes in loose natural curls of the kind that made me slightly jealous. The sooty-gray pantsuit complemented her ivory skin. "Do you mind watching little Timmy for a while?"

I glanced over at her son and smiled. He'd already made himself at home in the shop and stole everyone's heart with his adorable dimples, his sheriff's star pin stuck to his shirt, and the cowboy hat that dangled from a lanyard down his back. "He's always welcome here," I said.

The bell over the front door dinged as the door opened. An early-summer scent filtered through—it was a combination of the Lake Honey Springs, mixed with the wood planks along Honey Springs Pier and a hint of boat diesel. It wouldn't be long until these early mornings in the shop were filled with tourists who called Honey Springs their vacation destination.

Lake Honey Springs was wide enough and big enough for large engine boats, big game fishing tournaments, or relaxing in rented cabins with beautiful lakefront views. It was a magical place to live and work.

"I love staying with you, Aunt Roxy." Timmy's smile widened, as did his dimples.

"You like staying with Pepper." I winked at him and tousled the five-year-old's shaggy dark hair.

Pepper heard his name and jumped up from his bed next to the counter to scurry over for some pats and rubs. He was a very smart dog. I'd heard that about Schnauzers, and Pepper proved it.

The timer on my watch buzzed, and I hit the end button and turned to Debbie. "Timmy's a great help. And we could use a good sheriff around here." I pointed through the swinging door in the back of the coffeehouse that led to the kitchen. "If I don't get that breakfast casserole out of the oven, it's gonna be stinky in here."

"I'm off, then," Debbie chirped. "You be on your best behavior for Roxy," I heard her warn Timmy as I shoved through the door.

"You heard Aunt Roxy. I'm a good sheriff." Timmy nodded and followed me into the back.

The kitchen smelled of warm maple syrup and fried chicken, an addictive combination that was deadly to the waistline. The Bean Hive was first and foremost a coffeehouse, though, and nothing went better with coffee than a smidgen of food and bit of conversation. It was the chatter and laughter of customers that filled me with happiness. Knowing that I'd created something with my own hands that satisfied my clientele was my purpose.

Each week, I made a breakfast casserole for the morning customers, a soup special for the lunch customers, and a few sweet treats for folks who would swing in at odd hours.

"Good morning!" Bunny Bowowski pushed through the door with a grin, grabbed a Bean Hive apron off the hook, and replaced it with her brown pocketbook. I smiled every time I saw her in the black pants and Bean Hive logo tee that I had deemed our work attire. At first, she was very resistant to anything but her usual housedress and some sort of hat, but she came around to the idea. It was probably one of the best ideas I'd ever had, because it was a no-brainer to jump out of bed, throw on the uniform, pull my hair up in as much of a bun as I could muster with my mop of curls, and head out the door so early in the morning.

"Something smells awfully delicious in here. Is it you?" She leaned into Timmy, who'd found a spot on the stool that butted up to the steel work station in the middle of the room where I prepped not only the food, but crafted all the coffee blends that made the Bean Hive stand out.

Timmy laughed. "No, silly. It's her food."

"I think you're right. Look at these." I stood over the oven with pride.

Each single-serve cast-iron skillet had just the right amount of my chicken and waffle casserole, along with perfect golden-brown edges that would make any mouth water. Gently, I touched the top of one to make sure the casserole part had baked evenly. I felt Bunny creep up behind me.

"Oh, Roxy." She bent her head over the stove. "You've gone and outdone yourself."

I bounced on the balls of my feet, and a smile pulled up one corner of my mouth. "I think you're right." I jerked the towel from the tie of the apron around my waist and used it to grab the handle of one of the mini skillets. "I want you and Timmy to be the first to try one."

There was no arguing from her or him. "Perk of the job." Bunny joked.

Both of them followed behind me back into the coffeehouse. I put a mini-skillet on the counter and retrieved two forks and some napkins from underneath the counter. I left her there to help Timmy with his syrup and cut his food. I wanted to give her a moment with the dish so she could tell me what she really thought about the taste. Women in the south, especially Honey Springs, took their cooking seriously—it was almost as serious as church, and that was sayin' something.

I gazed around my coffee shop, with its exposed brick walls, original wood beams on the ceiling, and fireplace, all of which added up to create the cozy atmosphere I wanted for my customers. There were two large windows in the front that gave the perfect view of the boardwalk and the pier that led out into Lake Honey Springs. The few café tables inside of the shop were filled with customers. Even stools underneath the long window bar up front were filled with folks who liked to come in and read the morning paper while they enjoyed a freshly brewed cup of coffee.

"It's going to be a gorgeous wedding." Mae Belle Donovan held her pinky out as she lifted a cup of hot tea up to her lips. She was a regular morning customer, and she liked to hold court with all the other little old ladies in Honey Spring.

"Holding court" was just another way of saying "gossiping." Around these parts, gossip was part of the daily routine, just like getting out of bed in the morning.

"Hmm," Louise Carlton hummed when I passed. She brushed a strand of her silver hair behind her ear. "I did hear it was going to be changed to All About the Details."

"But my invitation says Central Park." Another woman in their group didn't sound so sure.

"Either way, Pam Horton is going to make a beautiful bride." The three women nodded.

Louise Carlton called me over. "Roxy! Is it all right if I come by in the morning with the new Pet Palace adoptee?"

"Absolutely." I patted her shoulder as I walked past her. "I look forward to meeting the fur baby."

Louise was the owner and founder of Pet Palace. It was Honey Spring's idea of an SPCA no-kill animal shelter. Every week, I featured an available pet to be adopted, and we had a one-hundred percent adoption rate, which started with my very own Pepper.

"I'll see you in the morning." She twiddled her fingers.

Out of the corner of my eye, I saw Timmy jump down from the stool. Pepper followed him over to the wood-burning fireplace. Even though it was going to be a warmer day, I still had a log burning for ambiance. On one of the two couches, two customers enjoyed their visit with each other, while Timmy and Pepper had decided to snuggle up on the other one.

I glanced back at Bunny. She flashed a big smile and gave me the okay gesture before she pointed to the waffle-and-chicken casserole. Bunny was older, and when she half-jokingly said she'd help out when I was swamped one day, she became my first employee.

I picked up stray napkins and cups left behind by customers on my way back to the L-shaped counter. I always looked at the displays to make sure they were inviting for customers. The four chalkboards that hung down from the ceiling added a nice touch of a homey, cozy feeling. The first chalkboard had the breakfast special for the week written on it, the second had the weekly lunch special, the third had a list of pastries and specialty drinks, and the fourth had all the business stuff, such as hours and catering information.

"He looks so much like Tim," Bunny said when I walked over to the tea bar next to her.

"I don't really remember Tim that much." I tried to recall the times I'd spent in Honey Springs each summer, but I had been so focused on Patrick Cane, Tim's brother, that I barely knew my own thoughts. "He's definitely got the Cane features."

I bent down and opened the door to the old dresser to get out the packaged sweeteners, creamers, and tea bag refills. The tea bar worked on the honor system, with a nice selection of gourmet and loose-leaf hot teas, along with an assortment of cold teas. There were antique tea pots from Wild and Whimsy Antique shop, which happened to be the first shop on the boardwalk, just in case a customer came in and wanted a pot of hot tea. I could fix it for them, or they could fix their own to their taste.

There was a coffee bar down the counter on the opposite end that was set up pretty much the same way. The customers would leave their money in a jar and be on their way. People in a hurry really liked this option, and it worked well.

The alarm on my watch sounded again, reminding me that I had an appointment with Babette Cliff at All About the Details, the event-planning shop a couple of doors down from the Bean Hive.

"Since he's so cute, do you mind keeping an eye on him while I run over for my appointment with Babette?" I asked Bunny, making my way around the counter to the freshly brewed coffee pots that contained the popular summer blend.

"Of course, I don't," she mumbled through a mouthful of casserole. "You've really outdone yourself. Savory and sweet."

I couldn't help but smile with pride as I made two coffees in to-go cups. I untied my apron and stuck it on the chair behind the counter. I grabbed my coat from the back of the chair and put it on. We were still having that in-between-seasons weather where it was cold in the morning but hot as a goat's butt in a pepper patch in the afternoon. "You are a dear." I kissed Bunny on the cheek as I passed her on my way out of the coffeehouse.

The voices of men yelling directions such as "go right! No, go left! Now forward!" echoed off the limestone walls of Lake Honey Springs. They were guiding the drivers of trucks hitched up to boat trailers and attempting to maneuver their toys into the water.

The boardwalk was starting to come alive with the early-summer tourists who rented cabins for family outings and long vacations at the lake. The boardwalk was a one stop shop for tourists if they didn't want to head into town. We had everything from restaurants to specialty shops for all of their shopping needs. The Bean Hive was smack dab in the middle, right across from where the long pier shot straight out into the lake. It was nice, in the late morning, to enjoy a cup of coffee while taking in the beauty of the lake.

The sun had come up and rested right where it was going to stay until high noon, when it would begin to work its way down the shoreline before finally ending in the most perfect blue-tinted sunset anyone this side of the Mississippi ever did see.

"It looks like someone needs a little morning pick-me-up," I said to Babette, the event coordinator and owner of All About the Details.

She was sitting in the middle of the large entryway on one of the two white couches. She'd taken pride in making the event center feel like a cozy home, as did the rest of our small town. The floor of the event center was gray concrete, but the cream shag carpet in front of the couches and under the coffee table made it comfortable. The folded-up quilts on the edge of one of the couches were a nice touch, too.

All About the Details was true to the name. The inside was definitely about the details of what the shop was about. When you walked through the double doors, it opened into an entryway that was decorated with different items used at the annual Honey Festival that was just about a month ago. The three large, bright yellow and black constructed beehives on each side of the walkway that led down to a large ballroom that was the perfect spot to have a wedding. The tables had white linen tablecloths and about ten chairs around each table. There was a stage in the very front. The lighting was available in any color or multiple if wanted. There were place settings on the tables with fine china and stemmed crystal to go along with the cloth napkins and sterling silverware.

"I'm going to need more than a cup of coffee," Babette said, barely looking up from the coffee table she was hunched over. "I'm not sure who's getting married to Truman Phillips, Pam Horton or Hillary Canter." She ran her hand over her hair and pulled down her ponytail. She paused then took another stab at gathering the messy mass of blonde into a knot on the top of her head. "I really need this event, financially speaking."

"I can guarantee this will help." I held out the hot to-go cup of coffee with the Bean Hive Coffee House logo printed on it. "It's my new summer blend. Out today." I was really proud of the logo. In the center was a honey bee with a coffee bean as the body. It was adorable.

Babette took the coffee. A sense of joyfulness filled my soul as I watched her jaw relax before she took a sip.

"You just might be right. This is delicious, Roxy." She took another sip and slipped her flats off her feet, digging her toes into the shag carpet. "Where are my manners?" She moved the bridal books that sat next to her and patted the couch. "Sit, please. I can use the distraction."

"What's going on?" I sat down and looked at a three-ring binder that was filled with all sorts of clippings, photos, and notes—and not in an orderly fashion. *The Phillips's Wedding* was printed along the spine of the binder, but it was a far cry from the work I'd seen out of Babette in the past.

"This wedding was all the talk this morning during Mae Belle's court session." I unzipped my light coat and put on the back of the couch. "Apparently, there's been a mix-up with the venue."

"I thought it was going to be the best event in my portfolio. I just adore Pam Horton and Truman Phillips. Their families are amazing, and there's no real budget." She pulled a photo of a cake from the binder and handed it to me. "Look at this cake. Beautiful. Almost too pretty to cut."

My jaw dropped. "Wow. Look at all the pearls. Who on earth is going to make this around here?"

"Emily Rich over at The Bee's Knees Bakery." She caught me off guard. Really off guard.

"Are you sure?" I asked. "She just opened, and I don't think she's ever done anything so elaborate."

It wasn't that Emily Rich wasn't a great baker. She was. In fact, I was instrumental in her opening The Bee's Knees Bakery after she graduated from high school and worked a summer for me.

As most parents did, her parents wanted Emily to go to college and fulfill her career dreams the educational way. Emily had other plans. She was a whiz in the kitchen, and when she worked in my coffee house —where I did make some basic pastries to go with the coffee—she went above and beyond with amazing desserts that I never wanted to make.

She was still new and had very little formal training. I hated to see her take on a much bigger project than she could handle, because that could be a downfall of a business. I knew that because of the coffee house. The worst thing for a new business was a bad review, especially in a small town like Honey Springs.

"It's not Pam who wants this cake. It's Hillary Canter." Babette rolled her eyes so hard, it looked like she hurt herself. "I'm supposed to meet with Emily this afternoon to show her the photo. I hope she can do it, because Hillary has no problem firing her and getting a new baker."

"I thought we were talking about the Phillips's wedding." I hesitated, blinking and baffled. "Who is Hillary Canter?" I asked since she'd mentioned her a couple of times.

"Oh, I forget that you didn't grow up here." She shook her head. The messy bun toppled to the right, and the ponytail holder dropped onto the shag rug when she bent over to look through the binder.

"Meet Hillary Canter." Babette shoved a photo of a woman about our age in a two-piece cream suit, wearing a feather head topper and with a glass of white wine in her hand. Her long black hair cascaded down her right shoulder.

"No teeth?" I questioned.

"Of course, she has teeth." Babette moved the photo so she could see it. "Beautiful teeth. Amazing body. Money. And she's Pam's best friend."

"I mean she doesn't smile with an open grin." Not that it was bad, but when a southerner didn't smile with a big, wide smile, it seemed like she was hiding something. My aunt Maxi told me to smile and smile bigger every time she took a picture of me. Once, she told me that she didn't trust a woman who didn't smile without her teeth showing. "Never mind." I waved it off.

"You'd think *she* was getting married," she said with a raised eyebrow. She shoved the photo back into the binder, flipped the pages a couple of times, and took out a clipping of another cake, a simple four-layer white cake with pink and yellow roses lining each layer. It was beautiful, and it was definitely more along the lines of what Emily could do.

Babette let out a long sigh. "Now that the wedding is right around the corner, Pam is listening more to Hillary. She's wondering if Hillary is right about the wedding guests and how they are expecting fancy and not simple."

"I love a nice and simple wedding." My insides warmed, and I touched my ring finger, which had my engagement ring on it. "Lake Honey Springs pier has the perfect backdrop to make for an elegant wedding." I shrugged. "I think the bride and groom are the centerpiece, not some silly, fancy cake."

"Are you thinking of the wedding you've envisioned for you and Patrick?" There was a wry grin on her face as she stared at me, waiting for my answer.

"Ever since the fire, we put any talks about a wedding on the back burner," I said, remembering a few short months ago when my Christmas tree had caught fire and burned down a portion of my cabin. "I've been so busy with the remodel, and Patrick knew I was stressed."

"I'm so glad that you finally reconnected with him," she said, taking another sip of her coffee. "I remember when we were in high school and you'd go back home from summer break. He was lovesick for months."

"You think he was," I laughed remembering how I'd met Patrick Cane as a young teenager when he came with his daddy to fix something at Aunt Maxi's house. My heart still fluttered when I saw him with a hammer. "I was a girl. My poor parents."

"Years later, here you are." Her chest heaved as she took in a big breath. "And I've got to make a dreaded call to Pam to figure out what she's going to do. Tomorrow is the deadline for any sort of changes, and right now"—she shook her head—"there's nothing set in stone for her big day, and I'm getting very frustrated."

"Well, I hope I could bring you a little joy with the coffee." I pulled my jacket back on. "What was it that you wanted to see me about today?"

"You know." She looked as though a light bulb had gone off in her head. She bent back over the wedding binder and flipped more pages. She pointed at the page she ended up on and tapped it with her nail. "I completely forgot, but in the early stages of planning, Pam asked for a fancy coffee bar."

She flipped the big binder to the front and drew her finger down the very first page, which appeared to be a list of sorts.

"Keep in mind, this was before Pam let Hillary get involved." The tone in her voice changed from upbeat and high, to low and snarling. "Like I said, I'm meeting with Pam, and we are going to discuss my meeting with Emily about the cake. I'll remind her about how she asked about a coffee bar. Why don't you just so happen to bring me a couple of to-go cups of this amazing summer brew?"

"Nine a.m.?" I asked, knowing that was a good time to leave Bunny after the rush of the morning crowd.

"Nine a.m.," she confirmed, standing up alongside me.

"I'll be here." We shook hands, and I made a mental note to put it on the calendar as soon as I walked back to the coffee house.

"What was it that you came by for again?" She asked.

"We were going to discuss some joint events, but it looks like your plate is full." My stomach rumbled to life. "Besides, I've got to get back and get ready for the lunch customers."

She held the cup up in the air as a sort of cheers, thanking me. "Do I taste a hint of strawberries?" she asked after taking another sip. "It's so frothy."

"Strawberries, rhubarb, orange, even some chocolate." I smiled and zipped up the light coat. I didn't tell her the rest of the recipe. Some things were meant to be kept a secret, even in Honey Springs.

CHAPTER TWO

*L*ake Honey Springs bobbed with a few waves from the no-wake zone that extended from each end of the boardwalk. With the sun beating down at full strength, the boaters and tourists were everywhere.

The boardwalk had almost reached its one-year anniversary of the new renovations, which had provided a much-needed economic boost. From what my mama had said, almost all of the cabin rentals were filled. Patrick's construction company, Cane Contractors, was busy as all get out with jobs from locals who owned and rented cabins for income and needed to bring their cabins out of winterizing.

I did a little window shopping at Queen for the Day, the bridal and women's boutique that was located between the Bean Hive and All About the Details. Not that I had any place to go all dressed up, but it was nice to look.

From the outside looking in, I noticed Pam Horton, the soon-to-be bride, standing in front of a mirror in what looked to be a two-piece suit. But it looked like every other person in there was fawning over Hillary Canter. At least it looked like the Hillary Canter from the photo that Babette had showed me.

Pam caught me staring at her. She gave a faint smile with an even weaker wave. With a big smile on my face, I gave her a big wave, held up my coffee cup, and pointed to the coffee shop, waving her a gesture to come by. She slid her gaze over to Hillary then back to me, offering me a big nod.

I gave a last wave and headed next door. I might've been a little biased, but the smell coming out of my shop was better than any smell coming out of any shop on the boardwalk. The scent of cinnamon, sugar, and vanilla bean mixed with warm, roasted coffee rushed out of the door when I opened it.

There was never a better feeling than stepping into the coffee house and seeing what I'd imagined come to life. I loved being a lawyer, but I loved filling people's souls with happiness even more.

"Hi, Pepper." I bent down when I felt my fur baby. He nudged my leg with his nose. I rubbed my hand over his salt-and-pepper fur and looked into his big brown eyes. His cute and fuzzy mustache tickled my face as he gave me a kiss. "You're a good boy."

"How was Babette?" Bunny asked from behind the counter, which she was wiping with a rag. The Bean Hive apron was tied tightly around her girth—she was such a grandmotherly figure.

"She was good. She's busy with the Phillips's wedding." I gave little information because I could tell she was fishing for some good gossip.

"Hi, Aunt Roxy." Timmy had a broom pan in his hand. "I've been workin'." He yawned.

"You have?" I looked at Bunny with big eyes.

"What? He wanted to help and I needed it. Those early morning people are half asleep when they come in here. They make a mess spilling coffee and crumbs all over. I bet they don't treat their houses that way," she grumbled under her breath and made her way over to a table to clean it off.

Before she put the salt and pepper shakers back in the middle of the table, she polished the cow-shaped dairy creamer holders that I'd gotten from Wild and Whimsy Antique then rubbed her hands on her apron. "I've put in a couple more of the coffee-mocha Bundt cakes in the oven because those slices are going fast."

"Thank you so much," I said, guiding a very sleepy little boy over to one of the couches.

Timmy fussed when he realized what I was doing, but he climbed up on the couch, and I swear he was asleep before his head hit the cushion. His little sheriff's badge fell on the floor. I picked it up and stuck it in my pocket. I took one of the quilts off of the old wooden ladder I used for a couple of blankets and as a magazine rack and draped it over him.

Pepper jumped up and curled his furry little body into the bend of Timmy's legs.

"See? I wore him out for you." Bunny chuckled. "Now you can get more work done."

I glanced over the glass counter in the back of the shop and noticed that I needed to refill the goodies. "It looks like I need to amp up my production with the tourists back in town," I said.

"They seem to get here earlier and earlier each year." Bunny made a very good observation.

"I don't blame them. When I would come to spend my summers with Aunt Maxi, I thought Honey Springs was a slice right out of heaven." I let out a long happy sigh.

"Have you got this week's lunch menu ready to go?" she asked, standing over the tea bar. She bent down, opened the two front doors of the cabinet, and refilled the items that needed it. She was quick to refill, clean, and do anything around the shop.

"I do." I wiggled my brows. "You think the chicken and waffles was good, wait until you taste the sunny summer soup."

Just the sound of it put a smile on both of our faces.

"I wanted something that I could easily unthaw in a pot because I'm going to be spending every night this week just being in my cabin." I tried not to show too much excitement, but I couldn't stop my grin from rolling my lips over my teeth.

"Tonight's the night, huh?" Bunny asked, clasping her hands together. "I just love working here and keeping up with you young whippersnappers." She stood up and waddled back to the counter. She didn't need the money I paid her. She claimed she just liked getting out of the house in the morning knowing she had someplace to go. It was a perfect union between us.

"I love having you." I turned, poured two cups of the Bean Hive's Highlander grog, and leaned on the counter, pushing one to Bunny. We stood there in silence enjoying our drinks. I looked out over the shop at the wooden-pallet furniture, comfy seating, and old pieces of antiques I'd picked up from Wild and Whimsy Antiques and forgot for a minute about all the cooking I had to get done. I was happy. Honey Springs had finally become my home.

"Are you going to the wedding?" Bunny asked.

"I wasn't invited, but Patrick was," I noted, taking another sip. "I guess I'm his other." I held my hand in the air and wiggled my ring finger. "Since I'm not from here, I'm sure she didn't invite me because she really doesn't know me." I looked at Bunny and smiled. "Though we are thinking about doing a coffee bar at the wedding."

"Coffee bar? Whoever heard of that?" Bunny held a hand to her heart. "Well, aren't you something? What is a coffee bar?"

"Apparently, Pam has." I shrugged and brought the cup back up to my lips. "I've read in some of the wedding magazines that coffees bars are just as popular as liquor bars."

"Wedding magazines? Have you been looking at wedding magazines?" The voice that come out of nowhere made me squish my eyes closed.

"I've got to start looking around to see who's listening before I open my big mouth," I joked, turning to face Aunt Maxi. I wagged a finger at her. "Don't be going and getting big ideas."

"What good is that ring if it really doesn't signal nothin'?" Her disapproval of my long engagement was apparent in the tone of her voice.

She used her fingers to fluff her short hair so that it stuck straight up. She lifted the front flap of her messenger bag and dug out a can of hairspray that said "very stiff hold" in bright-pink letters.

"Don't you spray that stuff in here." I waved my hand in front of my nose to clear the air, since she clearly wasn't going to listen to me. "Stop," I protested every time she pushed the aerosol button down. "If my customers want to smell hair products, they can meander right on down the boardwalk to The Honey Comb."

I sucked in a deep breath and turned to go into the swinging door between the shop and the kitchen. The glass counter wasn't going to fill itself up with goodies. Pepper scurried along next to me.

"I'm not kidding. Everyone that's gotten engaged after you has either gotten married, or is getting married, or has set a date. Can't you just set a date?" she begged as she walked on my heels into the industrial freezer. "Patrick Cane is still the most eligible bachelor until 'I do' comes out of his mouth. Without a date, he can't say 'I do.'"

"Here." I dragged a tray of chocolate-cherry scones that were a customer favorite and that I liked to keep on hand for times just like this. "Take those out there and put them in the oven."

Aunt Maxi lingered a second too long.

"Patrick and I are just fine. Now that the cabin is finished and I get to move out of your and mom's house, I'll be able to think about things outside of my living arrangements." It wasn't a promise to her that I'd make a date. It was a promise that I had more time.

"Your cabin is ready?" She asked and blinked rapidly. There was a little sadness in her voice. "I was enjoying having you stay with me, like old times when you were a little girl."

"I loved it too, and I really appreciate it." I walked out of the freezer with my hands full of trays of scones. "I'm so ready to get settled back in, and so is Pepper."

Pepper's floppy ear perked up when I said his name.

"Ain't that right, Pepper? Me and you want our house back." I sent smooches his way. He danced on the tile floor in delight.

When I looked up, Aunt Maxi had already put the trays in the oven and turned the manual click timer on. She looked at me with a sadness in her heavily-blue-shadowed eyelids. She wore red rouge in a perfect circle on each of her cheeks, and they looked like little clown noses.

"Stop it." I hurried over to her and wrapped my arms around her. "We'll still see each other just as much."

"Not with Penny around. She's been stopping by and taking up all your time like she did before the fire."

"You know me and mama. We can't be around each other for long periods." I gave her a good squeeze before I let her out of the hugs.

Penny Bloom, my mama, wasn't a big fan of Honey Springs when I was a little girl. She never came to visit Aunt Maxi with me and my dad. It was the whole sister-in-law thing—they never got along and were very jealous of my dad's affection. He was the perfect man, and I'd missed him so much since he died. It was comforting knowing that I was going to marry Patrick, because my dad knew him and they really liked each other. I couldn't help but feel good in knowing he was looking down on us with a big grin and a thumbs-up.

Regardless, Mama had decided to move here a few months before. She wasn't sure what she was going to do with her life in Honey Springs, but she found a calling in the real estate industry. She'd been doing really well, and it kept her out of my hair. She and Aunt Maxi had reached a truce. Despite their differences, I had to say that I was pretty proud of the effort they'd put in to finding a new common ground.

"Guess what I might be doing for Pam Horton's wedding?" It was something that was going to pick Aunt Maxi's mood right up. She loved to brag about me and the Bean Hive. After all, she did own the building where my coffee shop was located. All the marketing and business we could get was welcomed.

"Fighting for the bouquet?" She was relentless. "They say that whoever catches the bouquet will be the next to get married." She crossed her fingers and held them up in the air.

"Finger cross all you want, but I won't be in that ridiculous crowd to catch any silly flower arrangement. Babette Cliff said something about Pam wanting a specialty coffee bar for the reception," I said.

"Coffee bar? We live in Honey Springs. Not some highfalutin city like New York, where they pay way too much for watered down drinks."

Her lack of enthusiasm sort of surprised me. "I thought you'd be excited that people are recognizing The Bean Hive as a great choice for their catering needs and daily coffee consumption." I put out of my head any notion that she was going to understand.

"Roxy, Pam Horton is here, and she wants to talk to you." Bunny peeped her head around the swinging kitchen door before she stepped in. "And the afternoon staff is here, so I'm going to head out." She disappeared, only to pop her head right back in. "Debbie is here, too."

"Tell Pam and Debbie I'll be right there," I said. "I'll see you in the morning."

"Have fun moving back into your cabin. If you need help, don't call me." She untied the apron from around her waist and hung it on the hook on the wall. She grabbed her brown pocketbook off another hook and adjusted it in the crook of her arm. "I'm too old."

"You're damn right, you're old." Aunt Maxi took a sip of her freshly poured coffee.

"Oh, shut up, Maxine." Bunny glared at Aunt Maxi. "I might be old, but at least I'm not some bitter old biddy. And keep your hands off my Floyd."

"I don't want that old coot." Aunt Maxi glared at Bunny. "He's the one who wants me."

"Well, I never," Bunny gasped. She walked forward as though she was really going to do something, but we all knew she wasn't.

"Enough," I said, pushing open the kitchen door. "Bye, Aunt Maxi."

After I greeted the couple of afternoon employees, who came to work right after their classes at the Honey Springs High School, I walked over to a free bar stool at the window next to where Pam had found a spot. I wasn't empty handed.

"Hi, Pam," I greeted her. "How about a cup of our famous Spring Coffee Blend to go with this warm scone?" I asked.

"You're so kind." Pam's eyes softened, and the corners of her lip slightly turned up. "I'd love a cup. But I can get it."

To say that I didn't know her was not really very accurate. Honey Springs was small, and everyone knew everyone and mostly all of their business. Patrick and I had run into them a few times while we were out to supper, but that's as far as it had gone. It was most likely that

Patrick had been invited to their wedding because their parents knew each other or the Cane Construction Company had done some work for them.

"Don't be silly. It's a service we offer." I got off the stool and headed over to the coffee bar to retrieve both of us a cup, but not without going over to talk to Debbie first. She was sitting on the couch with a sleepy Timmy in her lap.

"You're better than any playdate." Her eyes softened. "It's been a long day."

"You doing okay?" I asked.

"Timmy's sitter quit on me over the weekend. I'm currently looking for someone." She shook her head. "Bliss of a single parent. I do all the work."

"I'm sorry." Though I didn't know her before I moved back and started dating Patrick again, I still could feel her pain from the loss of her husband. "Is there anything I can do?"

"Patrick is going to keep him a couple of days this week." She positioned herself on the edge of the couch before she jockeyed Timmy into position so she could stand.

"He is?" I asked, realizing I'd not talked to him yet, which was very unusual.

"Yeah. He said he's had to cancel a few contracted houses." She hoisted herself and a very limp little boy to stand.

I stood up with her and held my hands around her in case I needed to do some quick catching. She laughed.

"I'm an old pro." She winked. "You're going to make a great mother one day."

"One day real far away." I walked with her to the door and let her out of the shop.

I went back to retrieve the coffee for Pam and me. The usual afternoon crowd was starting to trickle in since school had let out. In came the parents who had dropped their kids off for practices and the high school kids that came in for social hour were my afternoon crowd.

"How's the wedding planning going?" I asked her, sliding the cup in front of her, careful not to spill. "You looked a little overwhelmed next door."

"That obvious?" Her brows dipped. She lifted the coffee with both hands. "I don't know. It's just not feeling like my wedding. That's all." She took a sip and then another. The pause between sips was apparently all she needed to just let loose. Her lips started going a mile a minute. "I guess it's my wedding and I need to take charge. If Hillary wants to get married, maybe she should plan her own wedding. But she's so bossy that no man can stand being around her. Truman and I never fight. Never." She shook her head and pinched off a piece of the scone then popped it in her mouth.

"Ever since I let Hillary talk me into the different cake, the different color scheme, and all this fancy stuff, Truman and I haven't gotten along. She even talked me into changing the bridesmaids' dresses because she doesn't look as thin in the ones I'd picked out," she mumbled with a mouth full of pastry. She swallowed. "I'm sorry. I shouldn't've unloaded on you, but sometimes it's good to tell someone who's just impartial."

"I'm sorry you're going through this." Apparently, it wasn't the time to bring up the coffee bar for her wedding. I didn't want to be like another Hillary in her life. "Is Hillary your best friend?"

I wanted to know so I could establish what sort of boundaries they had with each other.

"Yes. For years." She took another bite of the scone then took a sip of coffee.

"Have you told her that you don't want to do all those things she's suggesting? Because really, she's merely suggesting the changes. It's you that has to implement them." All of those years of law school did come in handy sometimes, especially the classes where I learned to listen to what the client really wanted. It was my job to come out of the court-room with more.

In my head, Pam wanted an amazing wedding, but she wanted to keep her husband happy and her friendship with Hillary intact. It appeared that she didn't know how to do that.

"No. She'll get mad and stomp around pouting. I hate it when she does that," Pam said.

"Why don't you sit down with Truman and go over the dream wedding that you two wanted? If none of those details fit in with what you've got planned right now, then maybe you do need to have a little come-to-Jesus meeting with Hillary and tell her what's what," I suggested, merely trying to give her power back.

It was good advice, and I could tell by how her jaw relaxed that she had become receptive to what I was saying. Plus, if they went back over the plans they'd originally had, a coffee bar might be in there.

Just then, the bell over the coffee house door dinged, and none other than Hillary Canter walked in.

"There you are." She tugged on Pam's shirt. Her long hair laid perfectly across one shoulder. "Honey Springs sure could use a Starbucks." She slid her gaze over to me. "It's not that your little shop isn't cute"—she shrugged—"I just like a nice cup of coffee. That's all."

"No offense here." I bit back the words I really wanted to say. Though I wasn't following my advice to Pam, it was my business, and it wouldn't look good if I got into a fight with someone standing in my shop.

"It offends me." Pam jumped off the stool and thrusted her fists down to the ground as she came nose to nose with Hillary.

It appeared to me that Pam had suddenly found her voice.

"You can't come into someone's place of business and say hurtful things. You have no idea how good this coffee is." The volume of Pam's voice escalated with each word. She flung her ring finger in the air and wiggled her engagement ring in Hillary's face. "This is mine. This wedding is mine. I'm sick and tired of you trying to make it yours. Maybe, just maybe, if you were nice or even the slightest bit kind, you'd get a boyfriend who would want to marry you."

"You ungrateful little nobody!" Hillary's nostrils flared. "You can never have the wedding you want without me."

In one fluid motion, Pam twisted around, grabbed her cup of coffee, and threw it on the front of Hillary's shirt.

"You. You!" Hillary's jaw dropped before her lips squished together and her eyes lit with fire. "You have lost your mind! And you"—Hillary hissed in a hateful tone, and she jabbed Pam's chest bone with her finger—"You can find another maid of honor because you don't deserve me!"

Suddenly, Hillary stopped. Her chest heaved when she sucked in a big breath. Her right eyebrow rose a fraction of an inch. Then, it was just as if the devil himself made an appearance right there in the front of my coffeehouse. A satanic smile spread across Hillary Canter's thin lips.

She cleared her throat. "I wasn't going to tell you, but in light of your lack of friendship and what you've done to me today, Truman made a pass at me a couple of weeks ago. At first, I thought it was just a kiss, but later realized he wants a real woman." She shrugged and slowly tilted her head to the right. "Sure, I resisted at first." She scrunched her nose. "But I too get awfully lonely and I'm a real woman."

Pam wasn't going to let that go even as Hillary turned to exit the coffee shop. "You are a liar! I hate you! You're dead to me!" Pam screamed after her.

"Are you okay?" I asked, ignoring the slamming shop door that Hillary had used extra strength to close.

"No." Pam shook her head and rushed off to the bathroom.

I stood there for a minute wondering if I should follow her or let her be. Then I decided that if I was in her shoes, I would want someone to check on me. My conscience was right. I headed in there and found her slumped over the sink throwing water on herself, but she wasn't alone.

Loretta Bebe, of all people, was slowly dragging her hand up and down Pam's back.

How did she slip into the coffeehouse without me hearing her? I eyed her suspiciously.

"Now, now dear," Loretta's southern voice oozed with comfort. Her words were drawn out with long sounds that made one-syllable words into two. Mr. Webster had to be rolling around in his grave. "It'll all be just f-iiiine." She patted and rubbed again. "You can take yourself down the boardwalk to Touched by an Angel Spa and get all these feeling worked out with a good mass-age." Loretta's twang made words sound so much more different than how they were supposed to be pronounced.

"Or you can get a spray tan. A little color this time of the year makes everyone feel so good. Not that I'd know." She drew her face up to look at her reflection in the mirror. Her very tan face stared back at her before she noticed I'd walked in. "Honey, my skin color is all natural, since I'm part Cherokee."

Yeah, right, I wanted to say, knowing that all the talk around town was that Touched by an Angel Spa had a running tab for Loretta and her tanning bed habit. If she wanted to think that everyone believed she was part Native American, it was no sweat off my back. Who was I to judge?

"Roxanne." She nodded at me.

"Low-retta," I said her name the exact way she pronounced it.

She didn't pay me any attention and went right back to rubbing on Pam. "Honey, we all get cold feet."

"Cold feet?" Pam's brows formed a V when she looked up and back at Loretta's reflection in the mirror. "I don't have cold feet. I'm trying to keep myself from not running after my ex-bridesmaid and choking her to death."

"Violence never solved anything"—Loretta smiled—"but vengeance is so rewarding." She winked and turned on the balls of her black flats. She stuck her perfectly manicured red fingernails in her short-on-the-sides coal-black hair and raked a few stray pieces into place. She stared at me as she brought her fingers to the corners of her mouth and wiped away any lingering lipstick. "Look at Roxanne here. She got the ultimate revenge on that ex-husband of hers by moving here and snagging the most-eligible bachelor in Honey Springs while opening up her little dream coffee shop."

"I'm not sure vengeance is a good thing either," I said, making sure Pam wasn't getting any silly notions from Loretta. Loretta was the last person on earth who should be giving advice.

"I don't know if your little spat had anything to do with that mean, nasty Canter girl, but I do know that her mama and daddy have spoiled that little girl all of her life. Damn near sent them into bankruptcy." Loretta's brows rose. "Now, they're so broke, they busted all Ten Commandments, if you know what I mean."

I didn't know what she meant, and I wasn't going to stand there and let her gossip about the Canters and their financial issues. It wasn't her tale to tell. Besides, Pam and Hillary were still friends. They were just going through a few growing pains, and that's what friends did with different seasons of their lives.

"Even if her parents are going through some financial issues, it doesn't give Hillary to right to just bowl over anyone she wants. Poor Emily Rich had brought some of her petit fours to last month's Southern Women's Club, and Hillary was standing in for her mama. She had the audacity to make fun of Emily and the simple flower Emily had decorated the tops of them with." Loretta pasted a smile of nonchalance onto her face. "Emily didn't let her get away with it, either. She stuffed one in Hillary's face. Hillary said that she'd not see the last of her."

"That's what that message was all about," Pam groaned. The corners of her mouth turned down. "Hillary called and told me that Emily was a fake and I really needed to rethink getting the cake from her because she uses box ingredients. Then, she threw it in there how you only get married once." She gulped and looked up at me. "Oh, God." She buried her head in her hands. "I called Emily and left a message that I just couldn't use her bakery."

"The nerve," Loretta spat. "That girl needs to be put in her place."

Loretta wasn't making things better. She was making it worse, and Pam cried harder. "I've got it from here." My lips formed a thin, straight line. "Thanks, Loretta."

"Mmhmm," she replied. "Any time." She waved her hand in the air. The stacked-up bracelets on her wrist jingled as she gave us a finger wave. "I'll be seeing y'all."

I waited until the door was completely closed to see if Pam was okay, because Loretta Bebe loved gossip, and I was sure she was standing outside of the door with a very curious ear to the crack.

"What can I do for you?" I asked, plucking a tissue from the box on the shelf next to the sink.

"Nothing." Pam took the tissue from me and wiped the tears from underneath her eyes. "Do you think what she said was true? You know, about Truman."

"Has Truman acted any differently?" I wondered.

"No. He just keeps saying that Hillary isn't the bride when I tell him what she tells me to do." She sniffed.

"I still think you need to talk to Truman about it. Find out if what Hillary said was true or if she was just nursing a bruised ego after you threw hot coffee on her." I winked. "It was the good coffee, too. Such a waste."

Both of us laughed.

"Did you see her face?" A little color came back into Pam's cheeks.

"Did I? It was great." I chuckled. "But I wouldn't take what she said for truth until you talk to Truman yourself."

"I'm not marrying Hillary. I'm marrying Truman. And if she's lying, and he didn't make a pass at her, I'm not letting her ruin my one and only wedding. I'm going to go home and tell Truman exactly what I want for our big day. You were right. We need to sit down and go back to what we'd planned when we first got engaged and what we'd envisioned. Not what Hillary envisioned." She wadded the tissue up in her hand and tossed it into the trash can below. "I'd not be one bit upset if I never saw her again."

So much for the still friends and all that changing-with-the-seasons crap.

She shook her hair, lifted her chin, and walked towards the door. She stopped with her hand on the doorknob.

"Roxy," she said over her shoulder, "would you like to do a coffee bar at our reception?"

"I'd be honored." I nodded and smiled, knowing that Pam was going to be okay, and I was going to rock that coffee bar.

CHAPTER THREE

"Are you sure?" I asked the salesgirl and twirled in front of the mirror that hung on the outside wall of the dressing room at Queen for a Day. "I'm not used to wearing a dress while I'm catering something."

Morgan and Crissy had come by the coffeehouse after they got off of work, and we enjoyed a cup of coffee before I got the big idea that I needed something to wear to tend the coffee bar at Pam's wedding, just in case the wedding was still a go.

Pepper sat on the floor, staring up at me. He always looked at me with loving eyes. Morgan and Crissy nodded.

"It looks great on you, doesn't it, Crissy?" Morgan stood behind me next to Crissy and stared at me.

"Fabby." Crissy's mouth formed an O. "And we can straighten your hair. It'll look so good." Crissy was always trying to get her hands in my hair. It must have been some sort of hairdresser mentality.

"Right, Jana?" Morgan asked the salesgirl. "It's perfect on her."

"Not only will you be representing your business, but you're also an invited guest," Jana said, putting a hand on each of my shoulders. Both of us looked at me in the little black dress that was much tighter than what I normally wore. There was something about a younger girl telling me that I looked good that made me instantly believe her.

I adjusted the plunging V-neck to cover up some skin that I wasn't used to showing then readjusted the sleeves.

"Honey, you could use a little help in that department." Crissy put her hands inside her bra and gave a little boost to her girls.

The sales clerk continued to readjust the dress on me to make it fit how it was supposed to. I couldn't help but notice her name tag.

"I'm just fine with what I was given." I nodded and wiggled my shoulders back a smidgen. "I think I'll take it."

"Great." Jana adjusted the dress again to sit a little lower down on the bust—too low for me.

"Good choice." Morgan nodded and slipped into another dressing room with Crissy so they could try on something they'd picked out.

"I had it on and just hung it back up." The angry voice echoed into the dressing room.

Pepper jumped to his feet, his ears back. He never liked for anyone to raise her voice. The sales clerk's eyes widened, and she hurried down the dressing-room hall to see what was going on.

"Then you aren't getting it, and I want it." Hillary's familiar voice pierced my eardrums. Her words sounded firm and final.

I peeked around the corner of the dressing room and noticed Babette and Hillary both tugging on a sleeve of a long white coat.

"I put it on the hanger to step back and take a look at it." Babette jerked the coat towards her. "Now let go," she demanded through clenched teeth.

"Ladies." Jana tried to calm the escalating tension between the two. "Let me have the coat before you two rip it to shreds."

Both women reluctantly dropped the coat into the sales clerk's hands.

"Now, let's see if we can be adults and settle it as such." Jana looked at Babette. "I saw that you tried this one on first. I'll just look at the size and grab another one."

"There's not another small." Babette's tone became chilly.

"And I can't wear a medium, but the small is probably too small on you," Hillary retorted in a nasty tone.

"Are you calling me fat?" Babette asked offensively.

"No. Maybe you are big-boned, but you certainly aren't a small." Hillary's voice was flat and vicious. "Jana, aren't you going to do anything about this?" Hillary put her hand on her hip and swung it out to the side.

"I'm. . ." Jana pinched her lips together. She appeared to be confused and upset.

"Yes. She's going to ring me up." Babette lunged towards the coat.

I hurried back into the dressing room and pulled the curtain shut. Quickly, I got my clothes back on, grabbed the hanger, and draped the dress over my arm. I didn't want to miss what was going on.

While I was changing, I could tell Jana was trying to find a resolution to the issue by telling the women that they could get the medium altered or even have the dry cleaners take it in. It appeared that Babette had tried on the coat first and had been deciding whether or not she wanted to buy it. Hillary hadn't tried on the coat, but wanted it.

"I need it for the wedding since it's going to be outside, in Central Park, under the gazebo, which Pam has always dreamed of since she passed it as a little girl," Babette said. It was obvious she was directing that at Hillary.

"Gazebo? Let me guess, she's now having pink bridesmaid dresses, too?" Hillary laughed at the thought.

"As a matter of fact, she is." Babette crossed her arms across her chest. "And they are going to be beautiful."

"Whatever." Hillary's voice dripped with sarcasm. "You can have that ridiculous coat. I'm out of here and out of this stupid town."

"Good riddance!" Babette called after her. She turned Jana. "No one would miss her if she turned up missing or gone forever."

Jana and Babette turned to face me when I walked out of the hall to the dressing rooms with Pepper trotting next to me.

"You just missed it." Crissy's eyes were huge, and she wore a giddy look on her face. "Babette just gave Hillary Canter a fit, and it's going to be all the talk tomorrow at the Honey Comb." Crissy twisted more than just hair when it came to gossip. She started as soon as a client sat down in her chair at the salon.

"I swear, I should've became a hair dresser instead of owning a pet store, because animals can't talk back when you want to gossip." Morgan laughed and broke the tension on Babette's face.

Babette busted out laughing. "She's something else," she whispered. "I had that meeting with Emily and Pam fired her from doing that cake all because of Hillary. It was awful. Emily was crying. Hillary is a disgrace, and I just wish she'd leave this town."

"When was the meeting?" I asked because I wasn't sure how much time Pam had after she and Hillary had their big blowup.

"It was a couple of hours ago, but Hillary wasn't there. Pam had said they were in a disagreement at the time." Babette looked between me, Morgan, and Crissy.

"Was that before or after the big blowup at the Bean Hive?" Morgan asked.

"Big blowup?" Jana asked. "I thought they were thick as thieves. At least, that's how they act when they come in here to get the dresses for the wedding."

"Pam threw a hot cup of coffee on her. In retaliation, Hillary told Pam that Truman made a pass at her." My words were greeted with gasps. "I tried talking to Pam and told her to talk to Truman. If there's no merit to what Hillary said, Pam said she was going to talk to Truman about what they really wanted for their wedding and not do what Hillary suggested."

"Maybe they do want a fancier cake, then," Babette said.

"Yeah. You're probably right." I held the dress out to Jana. "I'll take it."

"I'll take this." Babette tapped the white coat on the hanger.

"And I'll ring you both up at the register." Jana gestured for us to follow her.

"Great choices, ladies." Crissy stuck her fingertips in my hair. "Now, let's talk about what we are going to do with this."

"Later," I grumbled, pulled my phone out of my back pocket, and used the paying feature on it to buy my dress. I rarely carried a purse or other items now that my cell had almost everything I needed on it.

"Can you hold that until tomorrow for me?" I asked Jana. "I rode my bike today, and I don't want to go back into the coffee shop tonight since the high schoolers are working." I looked at Babette. "If I went back in there, I'd find more work to do, and tonight I get my cabin back."

"That's wonderful news." Babette clapped her hands together. "I still have an early meeting with Pam. We are finally going to finalize all the details of her wedding."

"You need to schedule a girls' night, since the cabin is ready," Morgan said. She was met with nods from my friends.

"I'd love to." I smiled and patted my leg. "Let's go, Pepper."

Babette, Morgan, Crissy, and Jana were right behind me. While Jana locked the door and flipped the door sign to closed, my friends and I said our goodbyes.

There was nothing better than living a short bike ride from the boardwalk. It was something I'd missed so much since the fire. Not that I was able to ride my bike in the freezing cold temperatures of the winter, but every chance I got, I liked to ride my bike. Pepper loved it, too.

Since the warm late afternoon spring sun was on the way to setting, I knew it was going to be a little cooler. I zipped up my jacket and picked Pepper up. I held on to one of the bike handles to steady it while I straddled the bike and placed Pepper in the basket that was strapped to the front. I used a little blanket I'd gotten at Walk in The Bark Animal Boutique, another shop on the boardwalk, and tucked it around him.

"Look at that." I let out a long and satisfying sigh when my eyes took in the beauty of the orange and yellow rays the setting sun had dripped over the calm lake. "I've missed this."

Another thing about having my cabin back was being back in my element and not rushing to a car just to drive to Aunt Maxi's or my mama's for the night.

"It feels like we are getting our life back." I checked on Pepper's safety one more time before I put one foot and then the other on the pedals.

The sound of the wooden planks of the boardwalk thumped under the bike tires. As I passed Bee's Knee Bakery, I could see Emily in there, baking away. It appeared that the supper crowd had already gathered at Buzz N and Out Diner. All the tables looked filled, a much welcome sight compared to the past few months when it was just too darn cold to leave the house.

Crissy Lane waved a pair of scissors at me out the window of the Honey Comb Salon. The freckles that dotted her nose gathered in a big lump as she scrunched her face into a big grin. Her freshly dyed bleach-blond hair was a sure sign spring had arrived, because in the winter she dyed her hair back to red. She mouthed that she'd call me later.

Crissy and I had hang out each summer when I was a teenager. She was a wild one, and I lived vicariously through her. Now that we were adults and lived in the same town, we hung out on a regular basis.

Pepper nestled a little more into the basket, but not without sticking his nose out into the fresh country air once we hit the curvy two-lane road that took us right to the cabin.

The trees were lined up like soldiers on each side. Lake Honey Springs ran along the road on the left, with beautiful cattle and horse farms behind the line of trees on the right. The leaves were almost finished budding and covered almost the entire road like a bridge, making it seem later in the day than it really was.

The cabin was up on the left, just about a four-minute bike ride from town. It was all I could afford when I moved back. There was no denying that it was a bit run down, but it was mine and with a little TLC, it quickly became a cozy home. When Patrick and I began dating, he was good about fixing little odds and ends. He knew I took pride in doing a lot of things on my own and figured I wouldn't notice things like a new roof or gutters, though I did and thanked him for everything he'd done.

My heart was broken after the fire. Buying the cabin was the first truly adult thing I'd done. Yes, I graduated from law school, which was no easy task, and I got married. It was as if I didn't let myself stand on my own two feet, though, and at times I truly believed that was why I was taking my time with marrying Patrick. I felt good about only relying on myself. Once Patrick and I got married, I knew it would all change.

When Patrick's company, Cane Construction, started work on rebuilding my cabin, I would stop by on a daily basis. Over the past month, I hadn't been by, because Patrick insisted he wanted the interior to be a surprise. I was impressed how even my mama was able to keep it a secret. Aunt Maxi, forget it. She couldn't keep a secret to save her own life. Patrick swore he wouldn't tell her anything or let her into the cabin until I saw it first.

The closer I got, the quicker I pedaled. The small cabin windows were illuminated with an orange glow from the inside lights. The covered front porch looked the same with the two steps leading up to it and the two rocking chairs on either side of the front door.

I pulled up and stopped the bike shy of the steps. "Are you ready?" I asked Pepper.

He licked my face and wagged his little stubby tail, wiggling to get out of my arms. He scurried around the yard, sniffing as if he were someplace he'd never been.

"Welcome home." Patrick stood at the front door with Sassy, his black standard poodle who was as much a love muffin as Pepper, next to him. He had on his standard blue jeans, cowboy boots, and T-shirt. Pepper darted into the house after he heard Patrick's voice.

I didn't blame him. Patrick's voice made me want to jump into his arms. But I restrained myself. "Thank you," I said and walked up the two steps to come face to face with him. "My mama's not here?" I asked.

"Nope. She was all set to come, but she said something about a client and a mortgage. She rambled something I didn't understand." He shrugged, his chiseled jaw giving way to the big smile that was always on his face. That smile sent my heart right on down to the tips of my toes. "It's just me and you and these ornery two, darling." He took a step out of the cabin and swooped me up in his arms. His lips met mine, and he gave me a soft kiss.

"Are you sure you don't want to run down to the courthouse and take my last name?" He offered the justice of the peace on a daily basis.

He'd probably drop me if I agreed, so for my own safety, I shook my head.

"I'm gonna keep asking," he warned. "Are you ready to see your remodel?"

"I could just stay right here the rest of my life." I rested my hand on his chest. "But I do smell something good coming from in there." I tried to sneak a peek over his shoulder.

"Don't you dare." He tucked my body closer to his. "I hope you like it. I worked really hard to make sure it was exactly what you've ever dreamed this place to be."

He gave me another gentle kiss on the forehead and brought my head a little closer to his ear. His warm breath sent chills all over my body, and the thought of spending every waking moment with that man for the rest of my life, nearly caused me to tell him to go ahead and take me to the courthouse.

"I love you, Roxanne Bloom," he whispered before he took two steps backwards into the house and uncurled me from his arms. "Welcome home, darling." He sat me down and continued to hold on to me when he felt my knees go wobbly.

"Patrick," I gasped, looking around. "It's beautiful."

I strained to see through the tears. The cabin was still the same layout, with an open first floor concept. The kitchen was located on the right, the family room on the left, and a smaller eating area toward the back. The guest bedroom was in the far-right corner along with a guest bathroom, and right across from it was my laundry room. Off the back of the cabin was a deck, which overlooked a wooded area that I loved so much—especially in the morning, when I would sit out there and sip my coffee.

There was a set of stairs that led up to my bedroom, but I had to see all the fancy decorating. Long gone were the dark, wooden cabin beams that used to be the walls. The walls had been drywalled and painted white. The open shelving in the kitchen had been updated, and the old, creaky wooden floor had been replaced with a light-grey wooden floor.

"I hope you love it." His southern voice was music to my ears. "I gave the designer all those southern home books you look at and told her what your favorite home-remodel shows are. She said you'd love the French country look, whatever that was. Now I see."

"The wood burner." I was so happy to see that they were able to salvage the fireplace with the insert. There was nothing better to make my little cabin more homey than a nice wood-burning fire in the morning.

"So, I take it that you like all this white?" He asked. "Even with those two?" He gestured toward the dogs.

"Even with those two." I pointed to his boots, which had mud stains around the soles. "I love all of it." I wrapped my arms around his neck and kissed him. "Thank you. I love it."

"Are you hungry?" He asked.

"Starving." My eyes grew to the size that I thought my stomach was.

"Good. I got takeout from the Watershed. I got you a big steak supper to fill that belly so you can get a good night's sleep." He walked out of my hug and into the little eating area.

The farmhouse-style table was set with several white candles and two place settings. He'd even brought our good friend, Jim Bean whiskey, to the welcome home party. He poured a little whiskey in two small glasses and handed one to me.

"To the love of my life. May we always be safe and warm in each other's arms," he toasted, and we both took a sip before sealing the deal with another kiss.

CHAPTER FOUR

"Good morning," I greeted Pepper, who'd found his way downstairs at some point in the middle of the night.

He barely opened an eye from his comfy doggie bed that was positioned just right in front of the wood-burning fireplace.

"It's early," I groaned when I noticed the new, big, wooden-circle clock overtop the mantel. The arms said it was four a.m. "At least we got half an hour more sleep than the last few months."

I tried to find something wonderful about that hour of the morning, when normal people were still sleeping. Owning a coffeehouse was not for the normal people. I grabbed the edges of my bathrobe, which I'd thrown on to come downstairs, and held it close to my chest. I gave a silent prayer of gratitude to the moccasin slippers keeping my feet warm as I walked over to kitchen counter and flipped on the single-serve part of my new coffee pot.

"One good, hot cup before we go," I said to Pepper, who was still ignoring me. Sassy had worn him out last night.

I padded across the room and stared out the back window over the woods. The stars were still out and dotted the sky with their brightness, but the rest of the land was dark and cold.

"I guess we'll have to see the sunrise from the Bean Hive windows." I relished in the feeling that Pepper and I had actually stayed at the cabin. I still couldn't believe that the new remodel was exactly everything I'd imagined.

Once the single cup of coffee brewed, I took it upstairs and got ready. It didn't take long to grab a quick shower. I pulled my long, wavy black hair up in a wet bun on top of my head since I was going to be making food at the coffee shop. I slipped into my black pants and tucked the bottoms into a pair of brown knee-high riding boots and a black Bean Hive tee. The only makeup I wore was some mascara and a swipe of some red lipstick. I was set for the day.

"Are you ready?" I asked when I made it back down to the family room.

Pepper stuck his white front legs out in front of him, and with his butt stuck up in the air, he stretched and yawned, finally bringing himself up on all four legs.

With the cup of coffee poured into my thermal mug, I let him out the door and went to retrieve my jacket, which I'd draped over a ladder-back kitchen chair. My phone started ringing, which sent my heart into a panic. No one ever called at this hour.

The phone screen showed my mom as the caller. Immediately, I swiped the phone to answer. "Mama, what's wrong." It was the first thing that popped into my head. My heart pounded in my chest and my palms sweat.

"I figured you were up, and I wanted to see how you slept on your first night back in," she said in a low and groggy voice.

"Oh," I sucked in a deep breath of relief. "It was good. I was actually getting ready to head on out the door to go the coffeehouse. Why are you up?" I asked because I knew she didn't set an alarm to call me. That wasn't her nature.

"I've got a real issue with one of my clients, and I've been up all night worrying about it." She paused. "Do you think I could come in the coffeehouse for an early coffee while you get the place ready?"

"Sure. I'd love company." There was something that she needed to get off her chest, and I was more than happy to have her unload while I was in my happy place. "Give me a few minutes to get there and get the coffee pots brewing."

"Sounds good, Roxanne." My mama loved to call me by my full name, and I didn't mind. It'd taken a lot for her to move here, and at first, I was worried about it. Now, I couldn't imagine my life in Honey Springs without her.

We hung up the phone, and I slipped my phone in my back pocket and tied the hood of my jacket snugly underneath my chin to help keep the chill off my wet head of hair.

I grabbed my keys off the kitchen counter and made sure the wood burner was cool enough for me to leave before I locked the front door behind me.

With no traffic on the old road back to the boardwalk, the bike light led the way with no trouble at all. Pepper appeared to sleep most of the way until we drove along the ramp to the boardwalk, and the wooden planks thumped one after the other as we rode our way down to the coffeehouse.

"Babette wasn't kidding when she said she was getting here early," I said out loud after I pedaled past All About the Details and noticed the lights were on at the event center. The condensation from my breath let off little puffs of air. "Babette?" I called out when I noticed she was sitting with her back to me at one of the café tables I had out in front of my shop in her new, fancy white coat. "It's cold out here."

I slipped off the bike, grabbed Pepper out of the basket, and put him down on the boardwalk. I walked the bike over to the bike rack next to Babette.

"You've got your new coat on." I tapped her on the shoulder. "Babette!" I screamed when she tipped right on over. "Babette! Help!" I screamed out into the dark sky, knowing that no one else was there to hear me.

CHAPTER FIVE

I pulled my phone out of my back pocket and dialed 9-1-1.

"9-1-1, what's your emergency?" The dispatch operator barely got her spiel out before I interrupted her.

"I need an ambulance at the boardwalk at the Bean Hive coffee shop. My friend Babette. She's not awake." My voice cracked. "I'm not sure, but I think she's…" I gulped and looked down at her just as the cloud that was covering the moon passed to give the moonlight a spotlight on her face. "Hillary?"

"Ma'am, what's going on?" the dispatch operator asked.

"It's not Babette. It's Hillary Canter. I think she's dead." The words leaving my mouth felt like an out-of-body experience. I bent down and felt for a pulse on her neck. There were no signs of life—no puffs of air like the ones coming from every word I took. She definitely wasn't breathing.

"Did you say the Bean Hive on the boardwalk?" she asked.

"Yes. Please send someone quickly." I stood up and walked backwards toward the railing of the boardwalk and looked out over the lake.

"Would you like me to stay on the phone with you until the sheriff gets there?" she asked.

"No. I'm fine." I bent down and clutched Pepper to me. "I hear the sirens," I told her. I hung up and slipped the phone back into my pocket.

I sat cross-legged on the boardwalk with Pepper snuggled in my lap while I waited the few minutes until Sheriff Spencer Shephard showed up.

"Don't tell me … You again?" he asked with his flashlight pointing straight at me as he referred to the other time I'd found a body. Okay, more than once. Make that a few times I'd found a body. "What is it with you and dead bodies?"

"I don't know," I muttered under my breath. I took another look at Hillary Canter while the officers worked on her. "Why does she have on that coat?"

"That's a very strange question to ask." Spencer's eyes flickered with a gleam of interest.

"It's cold. That's all." I grabbed the edges of my jacket and snuggled it closer to me.

It wasn't too long ago that I'd found another dead body, and I quickly learned that when you accuse someone of something they didn't do, such as murder, then you pay the consequences for it later. Though I knew Hillary hadn't bought the coat she and Babette were fighting over, it certainly didn't mean that she didn't go back and buy a different one, even though the store was closing and the door was locked behind me and Babette.

"What on earth is going on here?" Mama ran up to me, breaking the police tape. "Roxanne?"

"Ma'am, we are going to have to ask you to stay back," one of the officers said.

"I'll do no such thing." She fisted her hands and jerked them down to her sides. "This here is my daughter, Roxanne Bloom, and I'm going to be here with her for whatever this is."

"It's fine," Spencer said to the officer. He waved a hand at the other man. "They will stay right here and be out of your way. Right, ladies?" His eyes slid from me to Mama and back again. Both of us nodded in agreement.

The other man—the coroner—motioned for Spencer to join him. Their heads were stuck together as they conversed about something. They bent down, and the coroner pointed the pen in his hand at Hillary's neck.

"Who is that?" Mama asked. "Is that a dead person?"

"Yes," I replied. "It's a local girl by the name of Hillary Canter. I'm not sure why she was sitting in my café chair." I watched the coroner interact with Spencer.

"You've got to be kidding me. Again?" Her tone had changed from a loving mother to a scolding one.

"Don't give me that right now," I warned her. "It's been a rough morning."

"I'm afraid it's not going to get better," she groaned. "What are they doing?"

"It looks like the coroner is showing Spencer something." I turned to her. "Can you hang out for a while? I'm going to be crunched for time to open when Spencer lets me in the shop. Plus, I want to hear what you wanted to tell me about your client."

We watched the coroner take the point of his pen and move the collar of the coat away from her neck. I curled on my tiptoes, trying to see over the others, who stood around and gawked. Nothing. I leaned left then right to look around them, but still couldn't see a darn thing.

"I think this is the first time in your adult life you've ever asked me to help you." Mama put her hand up to her heart. "I really wondered if I was doing the right thing by moving here, and now I know I did." She reached over and gave me a much-needed hug.

My relationship with my mama had been a very volatile one, especially after my dad had died. I was glad we could connect, even if it was over a dead body.

"While we wait, why don't you tell me about what the client did?" I said. The coroner and his crew moved Hillary's body a bit.

"It can wait." She nudged me with her elbow when Spencer started to walk back toward us.

"Roxy, can I talk to you over here?" He took a couple of steps away from Mama.

I motioned for Pepper to stay next to Mama. She bent down to his level and pet him to make sure he listened.

"What's going on?" I asked when I stepped closer to Spencer.

He turned his back to Mama, apparently not wanting her to hear.

"Did you see or hear anyone running away when you got here?" he asked.

"Nope." I shook my head. "The only thing I noticed was that All About the Detail's light was on, which was odd at this time of the morning. I know because I'm always here around this time, and I'm always alone."

"Maybe you need to think about having Patrick drive you in the morning until we can figure out who killed Hillary." His words stopped me in my tracks.

"Killed?" My jaw dropped, and my mouth dried out.

"It appears that Hillary Canter has been murdered. She was choked. There's some pretty fresh bruising around her neck. At least, it's the preliminary report of the coroner, and he's seen a lot of these types of things. But we won't know anything for sure until he completes the autopsy." Spencer started to write some things down on his notepad.

The coroner got his church cart and started to take Hillary's body away while the officers roped off the area around the café table and down the walkway toward the opposite end, from where I'd ridden my bike not long before. Apparently, Hillary's expensive two-door convertible was parked down there.

"Exactly what happened?" he asked.

"What do you mean?" I gave him an odd look.

"How did you find her?" he asked.

"I was riding my bike, coming from that way"—I gestured towards the opposite end—"and I saw someone sitting here. Well, kind of." I hesitated.

"What? If you know something, you need to tell me." Spencer's voice was hard and stern.

"I thought it was Babette Cliff, from next door at All About the Details." It was as if my mouth had turned into a water faucet with all the handles on high. I vomited all the information. "Last night, she and Hillary got into an argument over that very coat at Queen for the Day. Ended up, there was only the one size. Babette thought she should get it, but Hillary insisted that Babette couldn't fit into it." My hand waffled in a back and forth.

"Kevin!" Spencer called after the coroner. He held up a finger for Kevin to wait a minute. "What was the size?"

"Small." I barely got the word out before Spencer took off in a jog.

"What was that about?" Mama didn't waste any time walking over to me. Pepper followed.

"He said that Hillary was…." I hesitated, taking a big gulp and licking my dried lips. "…Murdered," I whispered.

I wasn't sure if Mama was in as much shock as I was, but we stood there with just the air hanging between us.

Spencer said a few words to Kevin, then Kevin carefully unzipped the body bag, only exposing Hillary's head and shoulders. He picked up her head and peeled back the collar of the jacket. Both men started to nod. Spencer gave Kevin a pat on the back and a quick handshake, and both went in their separate directions.

"You said that there was only one small?" His eyes held a purpose.

"Yes. Only one small, according to the sales clerk. Eventually, Babette bought the coat, and Hillary stormed out of the shop." The sound of a door opening caught our attention, and we looked to see who was there.

Babette stuck her head out the front door of the events hall, made a strange face, and then quickly ducked back inside.

"Can we head into my shop?" I swallowed the thought that Babette had anything to do with Hillary's death.

"Yes. But I'm going to have to interview you later today to finish this up." Spencer pointed to All About the Details. "It appears Babette is already at work." He looked at his watch. "Five a.m. seems awfully early to be cake tasting, wine sipping, and making reservations for clients."

"She mentioned she was meeting a client early this morning." I shook off the chills that climbed my legs and travelled to my arms. "I really don't think she killed anyone."

"I didn't say she did. It's seems funny that the coat you said she purchased is on the victim's body. I'm wondering how it got there." He gave a side nod and walked away.

Pepper and Mama and me stood there for a few seconds. Out of curiosity—some would say nosey—I looked at Babette's face. My favorite class in law school was body language. I hated to brag, but I was definitely good at it. And Babette had a great poker face.

CHAPTER SIX

*A*s much as I tried not to look out the window as the darkness of the morning turned to sunrise, it was hard to focus on what Mama was telling me. The officers were taking pictures and collecting things in bags marked "evidence," In between, they did a lot of standing around.

Luckily, Mama had helped open the coffeehouse before, so she knew how to start the coffee pots. They began to hum and release the aroma that made the stress melt away from my shoulders and brought them back down from around my ears. I sucked in a deep breath and let the scent of the freshly ground roast soothe my soul. On the exhale, my brain felt calmer.

"She's moving already." Mama's words sounded like the cartoon characters who only made the wha-wha words. She continued to tell me about her client. "When she went to sell the house, she was told that she didn't have a clear title. I can't get answers from the mortgage company."

Pepper danced around his bowl. I walked over to the counter and pulled out the container with his kibble in it then dumped a big hearty scoop in his bowl. While he gobbled it up, I took a few more sips of coffee.

"I hate to do it, but I think I'm going to have to ask Maxine to help me, since she knows everyone." Mama sighed.

That got my attention.

"You must be desperate if you're willing to go to Aunt Maxi for help." I held up the coffee pot in the air, gesturing to ask if she wanted more.

"No. I've had enough. With no sleep over my client's situation and now this dead body thing, my nerves are shot. Coffee is something I don't need." She gave Pepper a few more ear scratches before she retrieved her keys from her purse. "This is how you hold your keys while walking to your car in case there's an attacker." She gripped the keys in her hand. One stuck out from between a couple of fingers as she jabbed the air.

"Let me know if there's anything I can do or anyone I can talk to for you," I offered, even though I didn't know as many people as Aunt Maxi. Since the coffeehouse opened, I'd gotten to meet a lot more community members and hoped to know everyone eventually. "Did you park near the hotel?" I asked, referring to the parking lot closest to Cocoon Hotel, the only hotel in Honey Springs that was located on the lakeshore.

"I did because the police had the other end blocked off. Why?" She asked.

"Do you mind taking the two industrial coffee pots to Camey?" I referred to Camey Montgomery, the owner and operator of the Cocoon Hotel, who had contracted the Bean Hive to provide free coffee to her hotel guests.

"Sure, I will." Mama waited for me while I grabbed the two carafes.

"Thanks, Mama." I gave her a kiss, and she took one pot in each hand.

"You're welcome, sweetie. Are you going to be okay today?" she asked as I opened the door.

"I'll be fine." I made sure to keep my voice steady so I didn't alarm her. She gave me a sideways glance that made me think she didn't buy it. I didn't acknowledge it.

"I'll call you later." She stepped outside.

I let Mama out the door and made sure I locked it after she left. Then, I headed back into the kitchen and flipped on the ovens before I retrieved a few of the scones and the Bundt cakes.

While the ovens preheated, I looked at the calendar hanging on the wall to see exactly what I had to make that morning. I'd marked that Louise Carlton was visiting to drop off a dog from the Pet Palace, and there was also a reminder to take coffee over to All About the Details written in black ink. It made me wonder if I was still supposed to take sample specialty coffees for Pam to sample. Standing around thinking about it wasn't going to get the shop open, and Pepper was good at reminding me. He darted into the kitchen and jumped up on my leg. It was his way of thanking me for feeding him.

"Do you want a special treat?" I gave him one. "You're so welcome."

There was nothing better than his unconditional love. That was one reason why I'd contracted the Bean Hive with Pet Palace, Honey Springs's local no-kill SPCA, which was run solely on donations and volunteers.

After I'd bought the cabin, I was a little lonely, and Aunt Maxi told me that I needed to get a dog. I had all intentions of picking out a bigger dog that would want to fetch and run alongside my bike—little did I realize that it was the other way around. The pet picks you.

Pepper wasn't about to let me get out of there without him. The rest was history. The thought of those sweet animals in the shelter put a spark under me to do something other than volunteer my time to clean their cages, feed them, or even play with them, even though Louise loved them all and took great care of them.

It took a lot of paperwork, coaxing, and free coffees to get the health inspector to even consider allowing me to have a weekly featured shelter animal in the coffee house to mingle with the customers, but the trend of service animals started to get popular, and it was my ticket to make an amazing proposal. Then, it took an act of congress with the citizens of Cottonwood, but it passed, and each week Louise would drop off one of the shelter animals to hang around the coffee shop.

Customers had the option to play with the animal or not, but I knew that if I could get the animals in front of people, I could get them adopted.

There was no better time to make my Cheddar Cheesy Fur Treats to pass out to customers who might have some animals at home. They might even offer them to the Pet Palace animal Louise was bringing. That way, I knew what was in the treats and they were very healthy.

"First, we will use the rolled oats," I told Pepper as I walked over to the shelf with the dry ingredients on it.

On my way over, I took an apron off the hook and tied it around my waist.

My finger dragged down the lidded jars that had the contents written in chalk on the little black label on the front of the glass containers. I juggled the oats, oatmeal, sugar and flour—all things I considered to be boring ingredients—all the way over to the workstation in the middle of the kitchen. As I made my way over to the refrigerator, there was a knocking at the back door.

"Hello?" I asked through the door after I detoured from getting the wet ingredients for the animal treats. "Who's there?" I asked, knowing that no one but the delivery men used that door, and I wasn't due for any sort of delivery.

"It's me, Louise," she called from the other side.

"Hold on." I rubbed my hands down my apron and unlocked the deadbolt and the other locking contraptions Patrick had put on the door for safety. "Hi," I greeted her.

"What on earth is going on out there?" she asked. "They wouldn't let me even walk up the boardwalk." The edges of her silver chin-length bob swayed back and forth as she talked. Her blunt bangs hung down over her eyes a little more than normal.

"Get in here." I opened the door wide to accommodate her and the carrier she had in her hand. I looked left and right outside of the door to see if anyone was out there before I shut it. "Do you know Hillary Canter?"

"Do I?" Louise let out a loud sigh that spoke volumes. "What about her?"

"She's dead." I gnawed on my bottom lip and looked at her with furrowed brows. "I found her," I whispered.

"Oh, no. Not again," Louise groaned. She stripped off her jacket and hung it on the hook.

"Why is everyone saying that?" I asked, as though I didn't deserve the response when someone found out it was me who'd found her. "I mean, she was slumped over in one of the café seats outside."

"She's awfully young to die." Louise's attitude from when I asked her if she knew Hillary had drastically changed.

"Murdered." There was no other way to put it. "She was murdered. At least, the initial observation from the coroner said she looked to be strangled."

Shock then fear appeared on Louise's face. "Who did it?" She gasped.

"I don't think they know, but there's been a lot of talk about her lately, and everyone's initial reaction was exactly the one you had on your face." I was getting a sense that many more than just Babette and Pam had an issue with not only Hillary Canter, but the whole Canter clan.

"Between me and you," she said, making my ears perk up, but she didn't continue. She bent down, opened the carrier, and tried to take a Labrador puppy out of the cage. He took her out, knocking her flat on her bottom. "Bentley," she scolded. "Calm down."

Bentley's tail was wagging so fast that it wiped the legs of the work station then thumped on Pepper's face when Pepper tried to get close to smell the new friend. Bentley paid Pepper no attention. He bathed Louise in kisses.

I had to hear what Louise was going to tell me, so I grabbed a treat from the dog treat jar.

"Hi, Bentley." I held the treat out in my outstretched hand.

It didn't take long for him to realize I had something to give him. Pepper stayed away from the smacking tail. Smart boy.

"Here you go." I pinched the treat in half and handed it to him a little at a time to get some more time with Louise. "What were you saying about Hillary?"

"That." She opened the flap of her bag and took out a file on Bentley.

The file contained all the information Pet Palace had on the animal, as well as how he got to the shelter, his previous health records, and his vaccinations. If there were any particulars the new family might need to know, such as behavior issues or if the animal is just a one-person pet, there was a detailed report in there about that.

Pepper stood by the swinging door, looking at me with his big dark eyes. He didn't seem to approve of Bentley for some reason. It made me pause, since Pepper got along with every animal, even cats. When Pepper went back out into the shop, I didn't try to stop him and make him sniff Bentley again. I figured it was best for him to do it on his own time and not be forced.

Bentley's attention span appeared to be super short, because when he noticed the swinging kitchen door, he darted towards it and out into the shop. His curiosity must've gotten the best of him.

"Oh!" Louise smacked the file down on the counter. "He's not really good at boundaries yet."

"Wait," I said when she started towards the door. "I'd rather him run around now and get used to the place instead of doing it when we are busy."

I had a sneaking suspicion that the coffee shop was going to be packed after the sun rose and the news of Hillary Canter started to infiltrate all the gossip circles.

"Are you sure? Because he's a handful, and I really need him to go to a family with children who will wear him out," she said. Based on the look on her face, he'd already worn her out this morning.

"I'm positive." I went back to the refrigerator to get the cold items I needed to finish making the dog treats. "Now, what were you going to tell me?" I grabbed the eggs, cheese, and margarine.

"I was saying that she'd gotten in trouble with the law once and had to do some community service." She held up Bentley's file, and I gestured for her to put it on the counter next to the door so I wouldn't forget to put it by the register. That way, when customers asked about him, I could just look in there.

"Like diversion?" I asked since I'd been a lawyer to many teens who'd found themselves on the wrong end of the law. Diversion was a program offered to minors, which helped to get them the help they needed, along with community service to get them set on the right track. It also expunged their criminal record and gave them a clean slate.

Unfortunately, I'd seen too many of those kids fall right back into their old patterns.

"Back then, it was just called community service." Her brows rose. "And her community service was to clean out the cat and dog stalls for a month."

It was an image I couldn't picture.

"She didn't like to get her hands dirty. I'd told her time and time again how she needed to do it one way because I'd get shut down if the cages weren't sanitized. She didn't care. She was on her cell phone most of the time. She didn't even show up one week. When I went to the judge about it, he said he'd take care of it." She scoffed. "It was then that I got notice that her community service had been filled, and she wouldn't be back. That's when I got my first taste of the Canters."

"She seems pretty privileged," I said. "Yesterday, I was in the boutique, and she was mad because someone took the jacket she wanted. She just wanted to argue."

"Did she fight with the customer?" Louise asked. "Because if that's the case, maybe that's who killed her."

"I don't think Babette Cliff is a killer, though Hillary did have the jacket on when I found her." I wondered how far Spencer had gotten with Babette this morning.

"Oh, dear." Louise knitted her brows together. "That's not good, especially with Babette's background."

"Babette has a background, too?" My jaw dropped.

"She killed someone. She was convicted, too. I'm figuring that's why she works for herself." Louise trailed off on a different thought. "Who'd hire a convicted killer?"

"Go back to the fact that she killed someone," I managed to say with a stiff lip. "Who?"

"Big Bib's girlfriend." Louise snapped her fingers a few times, and she looked up in the air. "What was her name?" She waved her hands in the air. "I can't remember it, but you can find out anything you need to know at the library."

Research was also something I'd been good at when I was a lawyer. I wasn't going to stick my nose into anything with Hillary's apparent murder. It was only out of curiosity.

"What happened?" I really wanted to know. It was a good time to listen as I mixed all the dry and wet ingredients together for the dog treats.

"Apparently, Babette has a little issue with anger." Louise opened the oven door and looked at the scones. "Do you want me to take these out?"

"Yes." I pointed to an open shelf that contained the cake platters. "Grab one of the platters with a dome, and put them on there." I went back to the mixing in the eggs. "*Had* an anger issue or *has* one?" There was a big difference between the two, and I wanted to hear the rest of the story.

"She and Big Bib's girlfriend had an argument over him." Bib was the owner of the marina that was attached to the boardwalk. "Around here, it wasn't unusual for kids to have boat races, and Babette and this gal had a boat race to prove something. I don't know what, but regardless, it was proven that at the last minute, Babette got angry that this girl was beating her. That's when she turned her boat into the girl's. The girl's boat flipped, killing her instantly." Louise's voice faded away, and so did the look on her face.

I gasped in disbelief. "Wow. I'd never figure Babette could do such a thing."

"Maybe she got mad about the coat thing and just went off," Louise suggested. "Back then, she went to a home for troubled teens, and we didn't see her again until she was a legal adult. Then, she kept to herself until she decided to open the event center. Ask your Aunt Maxi about it. The beautification committee was so mad that the real estate agent sold it to Babette."

I kneaded the dough for the Cheddar Cheesy Fur Treats and used the rolling pin to roll it out flat enough so I could use the small-heart cookie-cutter to get them on a baking sheet and in the oven. It was enough of a workout to let my mind wander.

"How did she get a loan with a record like that?" I knew from past clients at the law office that it was really hard to get a bank to approve a loan for someone with a felony. It seemed like discrimination, but private banks didn't have to give loans, and they could base their denial on many things. I thought murder would be one of them.

"Beats me." Louise shrugged and placed the dome lid on the platter.

I'd seen it many times before as a lawyer. After someone killed one time, it was a lot easier to do it a second time. I gulped and set the timer. My mind was such a jumble that I knew I'd forget they were in there, and they'd burn. Burning down the joint wasn't on my to-do list.

A loud crash came from the shop. Louise and I rushed through the door to find that Bentley had knocked into the tea station, sending a few of the locally made clay mugs crashing to the ground.

"Oh, dear," Louise cried out with worry." I'm afraid I'm going to have to keep him at the Pet Palace. He's not a good fit here." She pushed back through the kitchen door.

"He's fine." I played it off, but in the back of my head, I counted up the dollars he'd just taken out of my business. "I get a deal on these. If I put their business card out, then they give me a discount."

I tried to use all locally made goods and locally grown ingredients in the shop. It was my way of giving back to Honey Springs and promoting the small-business community.

"Do you really think Babette could've killed Hillary?" Louise came back in with the platter in her hands, her face almost somber. She sat it on top of the counter next to the register. They stared a coffee customer in the face. Then, their eyes told their stomachs how good a scone would taste with coffee. It was a fun marketing ploy that I'd learned from a coffee-shop barista I'd met in my previous life—that's how she'd lured me into buying hers.

I walked up to the front of the shop to retrieve the broom so I could get the floor cleaned up before I turned the sign over to open.

"I think we're about to find out," I muttered when I noticed Babette was standing at the coffee shop door looking in at me. With the broom in one hand, I flipped the sign with the other and unlocked the door even though it was a few minutes before seven a.m., opening time. When I opened the door, I noticed the sheriff's department was gone, and all the remains of the past couple of hours had been cleaned up.

"You're a lawyer, right?" Babette pushed her way into the coffee shop. She stopped when she saw Louise standing there, but not for long. Bentley nearly bowled her over. She snapped her finger. "Down," she demanded, tugging on his collar.

It was as if she were one of those puppy whisperers from T.V. Bentley immediately sat on the ground. His tail dragged back-and-forth on the floor and showed his delight at her presence.

"Good boy." She patted his head. "You're a lawyer, right?" She turned her attention back to me. "Because I need your help. I think Sheriff Shepard is going to charge me with the murder of Hillary Canter."

"That's not something you hear every day," Louise spoke in an odd-yet-gentle tone.

"Louise, I'm sure you can recall that my teenage years were a struggle for everyone around here. But I think my adult life speaks for itself." Babette walked over to the coffee bar. "May I?"

"Yes." I nodded rapidly. "Absolutely. Help yourself."

It was one of the reasons I loved coffee so much. It had some sort of relaxing effect on people when they came together to share a warm, freshly brewed pot. After my divorce, I'd spent many hours in various coffee shops, and it was then I found my therapy. I'd confided in people I didn't even know. Each person I met had come from a completely different background, with different socio-economic statuses, races, and even political views, but we came together over a cup of coffee.

That's when I knew how much a coffee shop could help heal whatever it was that was brought inside of the shop.

When I'd called Aunt Maxi and told her about the divorce and how I'd gotten myself enrolled in barista classes, she insisted that I move to Honey Springs to open a coffee shop on the soon-to-be-newly-renovated boardwalk. It had been perfect timing.

"I remember," Louise agreed, "and I do think that you've redeemed yourself, unless you did kill that girl."

"You've lost your ever-lovin' mind." Babette's face contorted into disgust. "I've paid my price for that. I've made a life for myself now."

"Unfortunately"—I bit the inside of my cheek—"when you're a suspect, all your history comes into play."

"Then you need to prove I didn't do it." Babette plunked down a wad of cash. "Here's my retainer."

"No. I don't want your money." My face softened, and I gave her a weak smile. "Why don't I get through this morning's rush, and when things die down, I'll leave Bunny here. I'll bring us a cup of coffee and we can talk."

I couldn't promise her anything, but I could listen to what she had to say.

CHAPTER SEVEN

"*A*re you sure you're okay?" Patrick asked, taking my hand in his. He'd gotten to the coffeehouse ten minutes after we'd opened. He wasn't the first customer through the door.

There was something about a murder that brought people together. Add coffee and some pastries to the equation, and there was a packed coffeehouse. I hated that the boost in sales was at the expense of Hillary Canter's demise, but I also kept a close ear to the ground.

If I was going to listen for Babette, like I told her I would, then I was going to have to serve up enough coffee to keep the gossip hot and coming.

"I'm fine. I guess I was a little shaken up about the coat." I sighed and pulled my hand away as I leaned my hip on the stove and stirred the pot of southern ham-and-bean soup, which I'd decided to serve for the daily special. It was perfect for the in-between-the-seasons weather— hearty, yet warm and delicious. Plus, it froze well in case I didn't sell it all, though I had a sneaking suspicion it was going to be a hit.

Bunny was holding down the coffeehouse. She would tell me if she'd heard anything that was worth hearing, for sure. It was practically her second job.

"You know the whole coat thing I told you about last night?" I asked.

"I remember. When I heard that Hillary was murdered, I couldn't stop thinking about Paige Lewis." He frowned.

"Paige Lewis?" I stopped the ladle in mid-stir.

"Paige is the girl that Babette killed." He said it as if I'd been there when it happened.

"The girl that Louise told me about." *Paige Lewis*, I thought to myself, using my remembering technique so that I would be able to recall her name when I asked around about her.

"I forget you've not been with me all my life." His strong hand rubbed up and down my back. "It was a big deal for someone to die, much less someone at our age. We were just sixteen, and Babette was the girl that always had a good time. She wanted something, she took it."

"She wanted Big Bib?" My lip curled at the end. My interaction with Bib had been brief since I'd lived in Honey Springs. Though he was harmless, he was a little frightening with his bearded face and unruly hair. Add his overalls and dirty appearance, and that qualified as a little scary. I couldn't see him and Babette cuddled up together, but who was I to judge?

"He was a catch back then. While I was working with hammers and nails, he worked on boats, building big engines and revving them up. Girls around here loved that sort of thing." The lines of concentration deepened along his brow and under his eyes.

"How come I didn't notice him?" I teased.

"Because you liked the hammer." He made a muscle with his bicep.

"You're a mess." I laughed and turned the stove down to simmer so I could give him a hug and send him on his way.

"You're trying to get rid of me." He pulled back and looked at me through his narrowed eyes. "What are you up to?"

"Nothing. I've got a business to run." I dropped my arms from around him and turned the burners off.

"You're going to snoop." He gave me a dark-and-layered look. "I can see it in your eyes. You're thinking about who the murderer could be."

"I'm going to see. Just check a few things out." It wasn't a lie. "I told Babette that I'd come by later today and talk to her."

"I thought we discussed this after last time." He fidgeted around so that he was in my line of vision.

"*You* discussed it last time. I listened." It was another trait that I'd kept from being a lawyer. Sometimes, it was better to sit still and listen. After the fire marshal had figured out my house was deliberately set on fire, Sheriff Shepard connected it to my snooping around about another case.

"Roxanne Bloom." His brow was high and rounded. "I'm not going to tell you what to do, but now that we are spending the rest of our lives together, I do think I should be able to tell you that I don't think it's a good idea to listen to anything anyone who might be a suspect has to say."

"I appreciate that. I'll take it into consideration." I patted his chest and moved around him.

I touched the Cheddar Cheesy Fur Treats that'd been on the cooling rack for about an hour. They were cool to the touch. I grabbed a few of the cellophane bags from one of the cabinets and put a couple of treats in each for the perfect grab-and-go for customers.

"Did you see Bentley out there?" I asked him.

"He's cute. He's laid up on the couch, barely giving room for people to sit. I thought he was one of those therapy dogs at first."

Patrick gave me a good idea. "Like an emotional therapy dog?" I asked.

"Any kind of therapy." He took the liberty to help me bag up more of the treats. "But I've been hearing more and more about emotional support animals for college kids and stuff like that."

"I sure could've used a support dog like Pepper in law school." I winked and rolled up on my toes to give Patrick a kiss. "But right now, you've got to support me and get out of here so I can work."

I loved how he always made sure I was okay and happy. He seemed to have taken that on as his life's mission after we'd reconnected.

After a few more tugs and pushes on Patrick's arm, he finally headed out of the shop. I smiled and watched him walk down the boardwalk, stopping a couple of times to talk to people. Then, I turned around to find Bentley. He was still sitting on the couch and taking up too much space. He was just a puppy, and I wasn't sure how long I'd be able to keep him from jumping around—and on people. I probably should have let him sleep, but I had other things in mind.

"Bentley." I gave a little whistle. "Here, boy," I called, patting my leg.

The jerk of Pepper's head from his dog bed next to the counter caught the corner of my eye. I gave my sweet dog a couple of gentle blinks and a smile. For some reason, he just wasn't happy with Bentley. Every other animal I'd featured in the coffeehouse, he'd cuddled up to and played with. Not Bentley.

Bentley yawned and stretched his legs out in front of him. His paws hit the ground, and his body slinked off the couch like a snake. He trotted over to me, his wagging tail hitting anything in its path.

I grabbed his leash from under the counter and clipped it on him. He jumped around in delight.

"Bunny, will you be okay for a few?" I asked. When she nodded, I continued, "I'm going to see Babette. I have an appointment with her and Pam about the coffee bar."

"I've got it," she said. "Find out what happened between her and Hillary." Bunny smiled. "This is the last bit of soup. Do you have any in the freezer?" She scooped some into a bowl and put it on a tray to take out to a customer.

"I do. It's in the freezer in the white tub, and it's labeled." I quickly made a couple of cups of coffee to take with me. I tugged on Bentley a little to let him know I was ready. "If you need me, I'll just be at All About the Details."

Pepper had me spoiled. Juggling a curious puppy and a tray of coffee wasn't the easiest or even the smartest thing to do. He'd jerk away to sniff something, and the coffee tray would jerk in my other hand.

Emily Rich popped her head out of the Bee's Knees Bakery. "Need some help?"

"That'd be great," I said with a little relief in my voice. "Thank you."

I was surprised that she took Bentley's leash and not the coffee. Anyone in their right mind would've been scared to try and hold on to that dog. He still continued to dart around the people walking down the boardwalk, sniffing the posts and sticking his nose where it clearly didn't belong.

"Who's this little guy?" She asked in a baby voice, the kind everyone puts on when they see a puppy.

"Meet Bentley. He's from the Pet Palace, and he's a puppy." I gave him an ear scratch after he came over to me when he heard his name. "He's very active and needs some training."

"Someone is going to adopt him," she assured me. "He seems very sweet. Where are you headed? I can take the coffees for you," she asked.

"All About the Details." I took a few steps with Bentley so my arm wasn't jerked out of socket. "I've got an appointment with Babette and Pam about the coffee bar."

"It was awful what happened to Pam's friend." I heard the words come from her mouth, but she didn't look as though she meant them. Her face was stern. "I heard you found her."

"She was sitting at one of the café tables in front of the shop." I glanced over my shoulder and looked at the empty chair. Images of the early-morning find replayed in my head like a movie. My body shivered, and I closed my eyes to bring myself back to the present moment. "I'm not sure why she was there."

"The sheriff didn't say anything?" she asked, and we took a couple of steps as Bentley led us down the boardwalk and closer to All About the Details.

"Are you kidding?" I had to laugh. "His mouth was clamped shut. They did all the investigation between the time I found her and the time I opened the coffeehouse."

"I wonder how Pam is doing, not that I can ask her. She dumped me like a hotcake after Hillary told her to." Emily rolled her eyes and handed me Bentley's leash. "Her family is awful. My dad talks about how shady her dad is, and after I told him what she did to me, he told me I shouldn't be so angry. But I was. I hate to be called an amateur. I studied in Paris. She's never even been there, though she wanted everyone to think she was so worldly... If you call going all over Kentucky worldly." The bitterness in Emily's voice was something I'd never heard before.

In Hillary's case, the apple mustn't've fallen too far from the tree, but who was I to judge?

"I'd better get in there and get the donuts to Camey." Emily referred to Camey Montgomery, the owner and operator of the Cocoon Hotel. It was the only real hotel in Honey Springs and conveniently located near the boat dock on the shore of Lake Honey Springs.

"I'm so glad you're doing well there." I was doing a small order of pastries for Camey's hospitality room, but when I talked Emily into opening up a bakery after she worked for me for a while and had gotten back from a pastry school in Paris, I introduced Camey and Emily. It was a big help off my shoulders for Emily to take over the order, though I still did the morning coffee for Cocoon Hotel.

Emily headed inside of her bakery, and I walked into All About the Details.

"I'm so glad you're here." Pam hurried over to the door. Bentley jumped around like a maniac. Pam grabbed the coffees just in time.

Bentley had jerked me forward when he noticed Babette stand up when we walked in.

"Hi there, Bentley," Babette stood with her legs apart and her hand outstretched in a stop motion. Bentley stopped in front of her and sat down. He lifted his paw in the air. "That's a good boy." She bent down and gave him a good rub, letting him climb all over her with kisses.

He was a different dog around her. I sucked in a deep breath and took the coffee back from her. "I wasn't sure if we were still going to sample some coffee, so I thought I'd just bring a regular cup so we could chat a bit about Hillary."

"I can't believe it." Her voice cracked, and tears came to her eyes. "When Spencer called me to see where I was all night, he told me that she was dead."

"They don't think you did it, do they?" I asked.

"I don't think so, but she was in my wedding, and we did have a big fight yesterday in your shop. I don't know. She was my best friend, and I knew she could be a pickle, but I just took her for what she was." She gulped. "I really didn't want her dead."

I couldn't help but notice that it was a clear difference than what she'd felt the day before. Then again, the day before, she was mad, and people say and do things to other when they are mad... like murder.

"Spencer practically accused me of it." Babette helped herself up off the ground and got Bentley situated on the rug next to the couches. "Have you thought about how you can help me with this?"

I handed Pam a coffee and walked over to Babette to give her coffee to her.

"Where is your coat that you bought from the boutique? The one the two of you were fighting over?" I asked, knowing if we could produce it, then it would clear Hillary from having her coat.

"I-I-I..." The corners of her eyes dipped. "I can't find it."

"What do you mean?" With a shaky hand, I handed the cup to her.

"I came back here last night to get some work done, and I left the coat here because I wanted to use it for the wedding. I hung it right there." She pointed to the coat rack she had nailed on the wall next to the front door and the display window. "Now, it's gone."

"Do you think Hillary broke in here and took it?" I asked, hoping that was the best scenario.

"I looked at the videotapes, and there's nothing there. Granted"—her eyes slide up to a corner in the ceiling—"the cameras don't focus on anything but the front door. No one else has a key."

"This doesn't look good." There was no reason for me to sugarcoat it. The facts were the facts. "I thought I'd stop by and see if Jana saw Hillary after we left."

"She locked the door behind us." Babette's voice was flat and sad.

"That doesn't mean that Hillary didn't go back and knock on the door," I suggested. "It can't hurt to find out, if you want me to look into things."

"You're the best!" Babette squealed and hugged me. "What can I do for you? I really can't pay you."

"Don't worry. I'm going to pay you." Pam eased herself onto the couch. "I'll find it."

I sat down next to Pam on the couch. The huge binder for her wedding was still on the table. "First off, I'm wondering if you can train Bentley for me. He seems to really have taken to you. He's so wild and crazy that I'm afraid no one will want to adopt him."

"He's really smart, and that'll be easy. Besides, I'd like the company and the security of knowing there's a guard dog here." Babette looked down at him. His little, tan body was curled up in a ball. His eyes were closed, but his tail was jerking as if he was dreaming. "He's adorable."

"That'd be great." That was a relief off of my plate. "Secondly, what do you mean you're going to pay her? Don't the two of you have a contract?" I asked.

"Yes, but Hillary's gift to me was to pay for the wedding outside of the down payment." Pam fiddled with the lid of the coffee cup. "My parents and Truman's parents can't afford to pay for a big event. That's when we decided to have it at the gazebo with a basic cake, and that's it. Then, Hillary offered to pay. I guess that's when she took the opportunity to plan the wedding the way she wanted it."

"Why didn't you tell me that yesterday after your fight with her?" I asked.

"I didn't want Loretta Bebe spreading the gossip all over town. But it looked like she ran right down to the newspaper and had it stuck in 'Sticky Situations,'" she said, reaching her hand out to the coffee table to pick up the newspaper. "I saw it in there this morning."

She handed it to me, and the first thing I noticed was that Aunt Maxi was the one who'd written it. There was a photo of the gazebo in Central Park, the park that was literally in the middle of Honey Springs's downtown area. The headline read, *Wedding Without A Hitch? Not in the upcoming Phillips wedding...*

I quickly scanned the gossip article. Aunt Maxi had added a little flavor to what had happened, and that's when I realized she'd not been to the Bean Hive that morning. There was no way she'd not heard about Hillary Canter's murder, and I couldn't help but wonder if she was avoiding me. I would make sure to call her, using the excuse that I was encouraging her to be nice to Mama when she called her about people in the community and whatever issue Mama was having with a client.

"I'm so sorry." I laid the newspaper back down on the table. "I knew Aunt Maxi had gone down to the paper and gotten a job. I just didn't realize she'd put something like this in there."

"It's not fake. All of that did happen. I just wished I'd been smarter now that Hillary is dead, because it looks like revenge or something." Pam took a drink. Those words coming from her mouth made her sound like a suspect.

"I don't suggest you say those words to Spencer," Babette told her. "After I told him what I'd said about Hillary and how I didn't like her, he really hammered me with questions. You don't have a past like me." Her words faded. "But I don't want to talk about that now. I've gotten very fond of you over the last few months while we've been planning your wedding. Maybe we can work out a payment plan or something."

Pam's lips rolled together, and she nodded. "If there is a wedding." Pam looked down. "Truman and I are going to have our big, long talk. But, as for now, I told you I would be here, and I'm going ahead with the planning as if everything is fine."

It was a bit odd that Pam appeared to have put all her ill will about Hillary on the back burner, and she was much more of a woman than I, given the rumors about Truman and Hillary out there, but it wasn't my story. I stayed tight-lipped, but not without making a mental note of how strange it was.

"First, I think we need to discuss the coffee bar while Roxy is here. What are your thoughts?" Babette asked, flipping through the binder.

"I was thinking it could be simple. We offer free regular and decaffeinated coffee, which I'll donate as my gift to you," I said, so the burden of having to pay that bill would be off of her. "I do suggest there be a couple of lattes and specialty coffees that I'll charge the guests for. Like a cash liquor bar, only with coffee."

There was worry in Pam's eyes. "I really didn't want people to pay, but I know now that I can't afford to not have them pay for extras."

"Pam." Babette plucked some of the papers from the binder. I couldn't help but notice most of them had scribbles and rewrites with Hillary's changes. "All the weddings I've planned have had cash bars. The regular and decaf is already donated by Roxy. If they want a specialty, then let them pay."

Pam nodded, but the sadness didn't leave her face.

"I'd like to set up the bar using the theme to your wedding," I suggested. "I'll even use the milk-glass coffee mugs I've gotten from Wild and Whimsy Antiques."

"I'd love that." Pam offered a smile and a bit of relief on her face. "I'd also like to talk to Emily again about doing the white cake I originally wanted. Truman and I are pretty basic. We just want to get married in front of our family and friends in our hometown that we love."

"I don't see why we can't pull that off in the next few days," Babette reassured her. She continued to rip out the pages that were no longer going to be used from the binder.

* * *

Pepper was one happy dog when he noticed I'd come back to the Bean Hive without Bentley. He bounced around and sniffed me. I could swear he had a smile on his furry face.

"I left Bentley with Babette Cliff," I told Bunny Bowowski as I tied the apron back around my waist. It appeared the crowd had died down, and a few tables were filled, but it wasn't overwhelming. "He really likes her, and she seems to really be able to get him to do things like sit and stay."

"Maybe she needs to adopt him." Bunny's brows rose.

"That's exactly what I'm hoping," I admitted. It was another reason why I'd taken him with me to All About the Details. I had noticed that

Babette and Bentley had a bond. Though she never led on to it, Bentley did. Dogs never lie. Either they like and trust you, or they don't. He had more of an affection to Babette than just trust—he liked her.

"Patrick called. He also came by to see if you were back yet. I told him to go on down to get you, but he said that it would wait." Bunny shrugged. "I think it was a little important because he was a little uptight."

"Really?" I was sure he was there to check on me about the murder and drive his point home that he didn't want me to look into it. "Did he tell me to call him?"

"Nope." She shook her head and walked over to the counter when a customer walked up. "I told him I'd have you call him, and he said not to worry about it."

The bell over the door dinged, and I looked up. Aunt Maxi was rushing in with a pink turban on her head and platinum strands of hair sticking out of the bottom.

"What on earth are you wearing?" I asked, knowing she'd give me some sort of off-the-wall excuse.

"I'm a serious reporter now." She brushed her hands down her pink sheath dress and the scarf tied once around her neck, which freely flowed behind her as she sauntered up to the coffee bar. "Do you have a quote about finding Hillary's body?" she asked.

"No. And I don't appreciate you putting that bit of gossip in the 'Sticky Situation' section of the paper." I gave her the stare with no smile that let her know I wasn't happy. "That really hurt Pam. You've got to think about those things." I walked over and stood next to her.

"Not if I'm going to be able to do investigating reporting. I've got to dig deep. If you think about it, Pam was the one with all the motive, from what I hear." She took the liberty to pour herself a cup of coffee.

"What do you mean?" I whispered.

"Now you've taken a sudden interest?" She looked down her nose at me.

"Let's just say there's more than one person who had very good motive to have killed her. I'm just looking around," I said nonchalantly.

"Who asked you to look around?" Aunt Maxi wanted to know. "Everyone knows that you're a lawyer. If someone thought they were in trouble, they're going to come to you."

"There are plenty of lawyers in town, but I can't tell you because I'm scared you're going to print it." I glared back at her.

"What if we work together?" She gestured between us. "I won't print anything until we have some real hard facts."

"You're ruthless." A smile crept along my face. "And that's why I love you."

CHAPTER EIGHT

The rest of the afternoon was pretty quiet. Bunny had gotten to go home, and the afternoon girls had made it to the coffeehouse on time. Since they were there, it left me time to get some more soup made and in the freezer, as well as some more scones. I also made pots of coffee to take to the Cocoon Hotel for the customers and staff to enjoy on their afternoon coffee-and-tea break while they waited for supper to be served.

The day had turned out to be very nice. The sun was shining, and a few boats were on the lake. Pepper and I walked down the boardwalk, and when we passed Queen for the Day, I popped my head into the door. When I saw Jana in there, we walked in.

"I'm so glad you're here," I called to her. She was taking pieces of clothing out of a box and using a steamer to get the wrinkles out. "New clothes?"

"Yes. We get daily shipments. Isn't this cute?" She held up a black-cotton bell-sleeved shirt. "You'd look great in it with your curly hair down."

"Only if I had places to go." I laughed.

"I've got your dress ready for you right behind the counter." She put the head of the steamer back in the holder.

"Actually, can I pick it up tomorrow? I've got to get these down to the Cocoon Hotel." I lifted the thermoses. "When I saw you were in here, I wanted to pop in and ask you a few questions."

"Shoot." She clasped her hands and rested them in front of her. "I'm not a stylist yet, but one day, I hope to be."

"I'm not going to ask about styling. I wanted to ask about Hillary Canter." When a quizzical look swept across her face, I continued, "I'm a lawyer by degree. I mean, I have a law degree, and last night, Hillary Canter was murdered."

"Pam's bridesmaid who wanted that white coat?" She drew her hand up to her mouth. "Murdered?"

"Yes." I'd forgotten about Pam getting her bridal gown here and how Hillary had changed the bridesmaids' dresses. It made another reason Pam would have had to kill her. "That's the one. But she had the coat on when she was murdered, which makes my friend Babette look like she killed her. Only I know she didn't." I leaned in and whispered when a couple of customers came through the door of the boutique. "Did Hillary happen to come in here and get a new coat?" I pointed to the box. "Maybe you had a new shipment in?"

"No." She shook her head, and her brows knitted together in worry. "I can't believe it. I mean, if she had the coat on"—she hesitated—"how did she get it?"

"That's the million-dollar question," I said. "Did anything happen when she was here with Pam?"

"She had the same bully attitude with Pam as she did with Babette. Pam just took it. Even when Hillary insisted on Pam changing her outfit, Pam was quiet, and her shoulders were slumped." Jana's eyes slid past my shoulders. "I'll be right with you," she called to the customer at the counter.

"Was anyone else around?" I asked.

"Just me and a few of the other sales clerks, but we didn't get into it. Of course, we have our own ideas of what looks good and what doesn't when it comes to bridal parties, but we found it strange that Pam didn't have but one bridesmaid." She shrugged and started to walk toward the counter. "I thought she was sad."

"Who was sad?" I asked.

"Pam." She walked around the counter. "It didn't seem like it was her wedding at all. If I hadn't known and she had been just a customer in the shop, I would have thought it was Hillary who was marrying Truman."

"Thanks for your help," I said.

Pepper and I continued down the boardwalk toward Cocoon Hotel. When we passed the boat dock, I could see that Big Bib had a few boats lifted up in their slips so he could work on them.

I still wanted to talk to him about the boat accident with Babette. It wasn't because I thought she killed Hillary—it was because she'd had already been tried and convicted of one murder, which would make it an easy case for the prosecution if she were arrested. I just liked to be on my toes and have a clear indication of what I could be facing. I needed to go to the library and do a little research so I knew what sort of questions to ask. If Babette was charged, I had to know her background. There was nothing more aggravating than a lawyer being unprepared and learning things about their clients that they didn't know until it was too late.

I got caught up in my thoughts, and it wasn't until Pepper darted toward the entrance of the Cocoon did I realize we'd already walked there.

The Cocoon Hotel was historic white mansion that was built in 1841 and been in Camey's family for years. Camey had hired Cane Construction to help reconstruct the old structure into an amazing hotel that was situated right on Lake Honey Springs, and they'd been able to keep the cozy character. The two-story white brick with double porches across both stories was something to behold.

"Good afternoon." Camey smiled. Her beautiful crimson hair was pulled back into a low ponytail. She had on a pair of black leggings and bell-sleeved black shirt that hugged her curves perfectly. The emerald-green necklace added the perfect pop of color to bring her outfit together. "You can take those on in to the hospitality room."

There was a food station in the room along with a couple of couches and a big brick fireplace that I was sure added light for ambiance. I replaced the coffee thermos from this morning's coffee with this afternoon's.

"Hi, Roxy." The little voice caught my attention. Amelia Peavler was standing there with a chocolate cookie the size of a saucer in her hand. There were streaks of melted chocolate on each side of her little face from where the cookie hadn't fit in her mouth.

"Ms. Bloom," Amelia's dad, Walker Peavler, corrected her. "Pepper!" Amelia bent down and put her arms out. Pepper gladly ran up to her. She let him give her kisses on her face, and he really enjoyed licking off any remaining cookie crumbs.

"Actually"—I bent down and looked Amelia in the eyes—"my real name is Roxanne. I want my friends to call me Roxy. Any friend of Felix is a friend of mine, so Roxy is just fine."

Felix was the cat from Pet Palace that I'd showcased over Christmas. Walker was in Honey Springs on some business over Christmas, and he'd had the same taming effect on Felix that Bentley had on Babette's heart.

Amelia came into the room and curled her arm in Walker's. "You're going to ruin supper," Camey said to the girl.

Walker had stayed at the Cocoon Hotel while he was here during the holiday season, and Camey fell for his green eyes and crew-cut blond hair. Amelia helped him seal the deal because she ended up loving Honey Springs, too. So, he moved them to our community, and they had fallen into place as if they'd been here forever.

"I just love these cookies." Amelia smiled.

"Oh, goodness." I looked at Walker. "Amelia is starting to look like you."

"God help her." He laughed.

Amelia looked up at her daddy with a big, wide-eyed look, as though she was trying to figure out what he was saying, and stuffed the rest of the cookie in her mouth when Camey tried to retrieve it out of her hand.

"It's so funny how Amelia can tell the difference in Emily's cookies," Camey said.

"What do you mean?" I asked.

"When Emily got here today, she was a little bummed. She said that this was the last batch that was going to be made with fresh cow's milk and butter from Hill's Dairy Farm." Camey frowned.

"Did she say why?" I asked, knowing that Emily had used Hill's Dairy Farm because they had the freshest ingredients, and it was a way to give back to the community.

"Something about having to compromise with cost." Camey shrugged. "It seems like I've been hearing that a lot around her lately. Business is struggling, that's all."

Walker put a hand on Camey's back, and I couldn't help but notice the look they exchanged. It was as though they were keeping a secret.

Walker's brows rose. "But she did say that she was going to be working at the dairy farm."

Camey corrected him. "She didn't say that. Hillary did." There was a hint of sarcasm in her voice. "Emily was very embarrassed and ran to the bathroom."

"When did all this take place?" I asked, wondering if Emily had anything to do with Hillary's death.

That was a hard concept to wrap my head around. Emily Rich had always been a sweet and kind girl who always was the first to help out if anyone needed it. Her parents were lovely people, not that anyone could truly judge her by that alone. I couldn't discard the fact that Hillary was mean to just about everyone she came into contact with.

"Two weeks ago, Hillary brought Pam and Emily in here to look at the ballroom for the wedding reception. I was surprised that Pam was thinking about changing the venue when she'd already sent out the invitations to Central Park." Camey wagged her finger. "Hillary had it all figured out—she knew how to get the change of location, but she didn't say that. The only thing I really remember her saying was to Pam when Emily had gone to the bathroom."

"Amelia, we better go. This is what we call 'girl talk,' and I don't want you to learn it." Walker slipped his hands over Amelia's ears and guided her toward the lobby of the hotel.

Pepper started to follow Amelia out of the hospitality room. "Stay, Pepper," I instructed.

"Go on," I said to Camey. "What did she say?"

"That doesn't matter now that she's dead." She tried to blow it off.

There was no way I was going to let that happen. "It does matter. There's a killer out there, and we need all the information we can gather." I gnawed on the edge of my lip.

"We?" Camey took a step back with her eyes popped wide open. "Don't tell me that you're looking at sticking your nose into yet another murder?"

"Not another murder. Just trying to help out someone who might be a suspect. I need all the information I can get about Hillary and how she wasn't so good to people, even the ones she cared about." I felt a softness to my smile, and I hoped Camey would see how sincere I was and give me the information.

She held the plate of cookies out to me. It was my signal to pour us a cup of coffee, since I knew it was the brew that was going to make her talk.

"She said to Pam that Pam needed to dump the Bee's Knees Bakery because Emily was just a child. She didn't do lavish cakes, and since the venue was going to be inside with white tablecloths and fancy napkins, Pam needed a cake to go with it. She said that her point was proven since Emily was having a hard time making ends meet and that she had to work at Hill's Dairy Farm. That's when Emily came back, and Pam asked her about it." Camey dragged the cup up to her mouth and took a sip, eyeing me over the tipped-up edges.

"She asked her?" I gasped in the amazement of the gall Hillary had.

"Mmhm." Camey nodded. "Emily was so embarrassed. She told Hillary that she hated her and she wished she'd drop dead."

I gulped.

* * *

"Drop dead? Are you sure?" Aunt Maxi was enthralled in the tale I was telling her as we stood in front of the microfiche catalog at the Honey Spring Library.

Even though Emily seemed to be high on my suspect list, I still needed to get the research for Babette's prior history.

"Yes. Camey said that Emily told Hillary that," I said, dragging my finger along the tabs of the years that went with the newspaper articles. "I wish they'd get these files on the computer."

"Honey, it took the beautification committee ten years to remodel the boardwalk. Can you imagine how long it's going to take to get these up on the computer?"

I laughed.

"Now, take Joanne Stone." Aunt Maxi's eyes slid towards the children's section of the library where the young librarian was sitting amongst a circle of children and reading them a story time book. "She's young and a go-getter. She's ready to get us up in the modern technological age. But not them old biddies on the committee."

"Maybe after you do your investigation and I find what I'm looking for, we can start our own library committee," I said. I finally found the year I was looking for.

"What are you looking up?" Aunt Maxi asked.

"What are you doing here, anyway?" I asked back.

"You go first, 'cause I've gotten something I think is going to be big." She nodded and narrowed her eyes.

"Very interesting." Normally, Aunt Maxi's actions didn't peek my interest quite as much, but the way she was acting caught my attention. "I'll bite. I'll go first. Did you hear about the fight between Hillary Canter and Babette at Queen for A Day?" I asked.

She nodded. "Of course, I have. I started to investigate the murder, but then something else got my attention." Her lips pinched as if she feared she'd say anymore. "It was over a coat, I heard."

"Right. The coat was a size small and the only one left in the shop. To make a long story short, Babette bought it, and Hillary had it on when she died," I said.

"Really?" Aunt Maxi drew back. Her eyes stared blankly at me. "Have Babette give you her coat." Aunt Maxi made it sound so easy and simple.

"She can't find it. She said that she took it at All About the Details after she bought it because she wanted it there to wear for Pam's wedding day. Her video camera didn't show anyone breaking in, and that's what makes her a number one suspect," my voice faded.

"That doesn't look good for Babette or Emily." Aunt Maxi's eyelashes drew a shadow down her cheeks. She was quick to dismiss my idea. "I've got something better." She nudged me with pride.

"What's better than solving a murder?" I asked, looking around to see where Pepper had gone.

It was way past his afternoon nap time, and he was curled up next to the card catalog.

"Figuring out what's going on with your mama's client's mortgage." She held a file in her hand. "I'm here doing some research on Bank Lending Mortgages out of Lexington. Ever heard of them?"

I nodded. "They are a huge lending company."

"I think there's some shady stuff going on there." Her brows rose. She leaned in and looked both ways before she whispered, "I think that they've either embezzled your mama's client's mortgage or they lost it."

"They're so big, I'm sure it's not embezzlement," I said, watching as Aunt Maxi's ego deflated. "It has to be an oversight."

"Why won't they let me in to talk to them?" she asked.

"You called them?" I stifled a chuckle.

"You think this is a joke, but I'm telling you I'm on to something. I don't know yet, but I am. I even used my Honey Springs Council-woman title. Nothing." She stood straight up. "If you don't want to help me, then I'll do it myself."

"It's not that I don't want to help you. I've really got my hands full with planning the coffee bar for Pam's wedding, everything needed for the Bean Hive, and helping Babette." A pang of guilt hit my heart as I looked at my sweet aunt. "Fine." I sighed. "You do all the leg work and bring me what you find. I'll look it all over and see if there's any holes."

"Great!" She screamed, and a big smile swept across her face.

"Shhh!" Dee-Dee the librarian warned, placing her pointer finger over her lips.

Aunt Maxi and I both laughed like teenagers.

CHAPTER NINE

The afternoon help was in the coffeehouse and taking orders from the typical crowd, along with a bunch of after-work folks who normally didn't come into the Bean Hive afterwards but wanted to hear the story. The tale of me finding Hillary Canter's body wasn't going away anytime soon.

Mae Belle Donovan sat like a little perched bird at one of the tables in the shop. Today she wore a bonnet that was tied in a big bow underneath her chin. "Don't you think it's a little strange that she had on the coat that she and Babette were fighting over just a few hours before she died?"

Mae Belle and Bunny Bowowski had been friends forever. The two of them had been regulars when I opened the Bean Hive. They were both on the beautification committee and came down every morning to see the progress Cane Construction was making on their approved changes. Rarely did I see one without the other, and both loved to wear some sort of hat.

Mae Belle had the same hairstyle and even the same pocketbook as Bunny. If I wasn't from Honey Springs and saw them together, I would think they were related. They acted so much alike.

"And with that Babette's past history," someone said.

"Now, now." Bunny Bowowski tsked from the other side of the table.

Bunny had decided to hang around after her shift. Her excuse to me was that didn't feel like going home to an empty house. I knew better. She and the rest of her little buddies lived for the gossip.

"It's time to put the chairs in the wagon." Bunny meant that it was time to go home.

"Who have you turned into?" Mae Belle asked Bunny. "Roxy, what have you done to my friend?"

"Why, what do you mean, Mae Belle?" I called from the counter, where I was going through the articles I had Dee-Dee print off for me from the microfiche.

There was really nothing in the articles that I hadn't already heard. They'd mentioned a few names of friends who'd gone down to the river to watch them race, but there was no clear motive. It simply stated that Babette and Paige were rivals. They'd agreed to settle the score by testing who had the most horsepower in their boats—and racing.

"You've somehow turned off the nosy parts of my friend since she's been working for you." Mae Belle's chair made a screeching sound as she stood up and scooched it back. "And I don't like it." She huffed and adjusted her pocketbook in the crook of her arm before she threw her nose up in the air and waddled out the front door of the coffeehouse.

"Why don't the two of you go on and get out of here?" I said to the afternoon girls. "It doesn't look like I'm getting out of here anytime soon. I have it covered."

I looked up at the clock on the wall. It was pretty close to closing time—six p.m. The last message I'd gotten from Patrick was that he'd be by the shop to see me, and he didn't want me to leave.

The girls were so happy to get off work early. After all, it wasn't every day I offered them the chance to go home before their shifts ended.

I'd sent several messages to Mama to see how she was doing, but she hadn't gotten back to me. I guessed that she and Aunt Maxi had their hands full, Mama with her upset client and Aunt Maxi trying to get the scoop. I was sure it would all work out just fine. From what I'd remembered from doing a couple of loan closings with Bank Lending Mortgage when I was a lawyer, they were always well prepared. Not that I did a lot of loan closings, but if I was available and needed some outside work, it was an easy gig. And some of that money helped pay off my law school debt.

As the clock ticked closer to six, the customers trickled out one-by-one and left me alone. I didn't mind. The sounds of the buzzing industrial coffee pots and the smell of some of the leftover pastries circled around me, causing my shoulders to fall back down instead of hovering around my ears.

"You need to go potty?" I asked Pepper, who'd been such a good boy all day.

He jumped up from the bed and darted to the front door of the shop. I swung by the fireplace and turned the gas off, so the flame would go out. The last thing I needed was the coffeehouse to burn down and the other shops around me to catch on fire.

I noticed the plates and coffee cups, not to mention the used napkins left on the tables. "We've got a mess to clean up. It'll have to wait until we get back."

I locked the shop door behind me, since I carried my keys in my pocket.

"Let's go this way," I said to Pepper as I started walking toward the Bee's Knee Bakery.

The light was on, and I'd not heard from Emily since I texted her after I left the Cocoon Hotel. It was probably nosy of me to want to know about her financial situation, but I took some responsibility in the fact that I was the one who talked them into opening it. To be fair, she didn't need the talking to—it was her father. If she was having money issues, I felt horrible about it.

Emily was inside, and she looked up when Pepper jumped up, putting his paws on the window and pressing his nose to the glass.

She didn't have any sort of seating in her bakery. It was just a come-in-and-order-or-grab-a-donut-or-two kind of place, or maybe cookies or whatever other pastry she had that day. It took her a mere second to come over and unlock the door.

"Hey, there." I walked in after she held the door open for me. "I messaged you today."

"Did you?" She forced a smile. "I haven't looked."

"You are very busy or awfully flustered." I noticed her apron was very messy—the inside of the bakery was, too. It wasn't like her, and it certainly was not like her to be so unkempt.

"I'm busy. Did you need something? You said you messaged me." She didn't move away from the door. And when Pepper nudged her leg with his nose, she didn't even notice. They'd been thicker than thieves when she worked for me. He even went to spend the night with her once or twice.

"Actually, I wanted to know if you knew anything about Hillary Canter?" I asked.

"I know a lot about her."

That wasn't the answer I was looking for.

"She's dead, for one." There was no love lost in her voice.

"Did you happen to see her this morning when you were here?" I asked.

"How did you know I was here?"

"When Pepper and I biked by, I saw the back light on." I had a sneaking suspicion that she was keeping something from me. "Listen, I know whatever it is that's bugging you isn't my business. I feel a little responsible that you're here. And if you're having some issues, I'd like to help."

"Did Hillary tell you about me?" There was even more disgust on her face the second time she said Hillary's name. "I saw the three of you at Queen for A Day."

"I was there getting a dress for Pam's wedding reception that I hoped would double as a work dress. Hillary was there by herself, and so was Babette. None of us were together. Tell me what's going on. I can help." I really wanted her to open up to me.

"The bank is calling in my loan on the shop. There's no way I can pay it." Her voice cracked. "I have all these birthday cakes to do, and I can't even afford to go to the Piggly Wiggly to get the ingredients. I owe Louise Hill money for the milk and butter she let me take on credit, and now I have to go in for her during the morning hours to milk her goats and cows to pay my debt."

My heart broke for her as the tears trickled down her face.

"Hillary Canter was right. I am a nobody." She buried her head in her hands.

"Let me tell you something." I put my arms around her. "You're not a nobody."

Pepper was distraught with her crying. He sat by our feet whimpering. When Emily started to laugh, she pulled away and looked down.

"I'm sorry, Pepper." She picked up his little salt-and-pepper body and let him lick the tears away. "You're better than any therapist."

"He is." I ran my hand down his back. He brought a smile and a happy heart to everyone around him. "He's worried about you, like I am."

"I'll be fine. I guess it wasn't meant to be right now." She sat Pepper down gently on his paws, and he darted off to sniff the crease of the door.

"Do you want to talk about it?" I asked. "Maybe I can help come up with a solution."

"You can go up against Bank Lending Mortgages?" she asked.

"Your shop's lease is through Bank Lending Mortgages in Lexington?" I asked.

"Sure is. My dad said they were the best, and Honey Springs Bank can't give me a loan because I'm so young with no real credit. He set it up and even co-signed the loan for me." This brought another set of tears.

"My Aunt Maxi is looking into them for my mama. One of her clients is having an issue with them." I ran my hand down her back to offer some sort of support, but my thoughts were somewhere else—such as the mortgage company and what was going on with them. "Can I tell her about your loan?"

"Yeah, if she can do anything about it," Emily sniffled. "About your earlier question about Hillary. I was here that morning, but I didn't see her. I decided to stay here all night and try to get as many baked goods done as I could muster up with few ingredients so I could sell them and have some money. I fell asleep on the floor in the back when I was taking a break. I woke up to a smoking oven with burnt cupcakes and nothing to sell when I opened the doors. By the time I got the smoke cleared, it was three-thirty in the morning, and soon the cows and goats would be up." She shook her head and rolled her eyes. "I had to go to Hill's Dairy Farm to fulfill my duties there. I left the lights on. I went out the front door, and Hillary was not there. I know because I would have seen her if she was." She pointed towards the direction of my shop. "I parked down that way, and I had to walk right past the café tables."

"You said three-thirty?" I asked.

"Yes. It was three-thirty." She didn't stutter.

CHAPTER TEN

"I'm telling you that it had to have happened between three-thirty and four-thirty a.m." I stood in Sheriff Spencer's office and talked so fast my words were slurring. I thought it was important that he knew the time.

He sat behind his desk and gave me the stink eye. "I thought I told you to stay out of it," was all he had to say.

The knock on his door came at the perfect time. I turned around to see a deputy walk in. He held up one of the mini-Bundt cakes I had left over from earlier. I'd packed them up with me when I went back to the shop after talking to Emily. "Thanks, Roxy," he said. "You've outdone yourself."

"Aw, thanks. Y'all always make me feel so good."

"Have you watched all the security tapes from the boardwalk?" I asked.

"Why? Why? Why?" He pushed himself back from his desk and threw his hands up in the air. "Why don't you just stick with brewing the beans? Why do you have to look into things?"

"Because I have a good friend, maybe two, who appear to be on your suspect list, and it's all because of a coat and a cake." I threw my hands up to match his.

There was a moment of silence between us. It was as if we were in one of those detective shows where the detective gives the dreaded pause to see if who he's questioning cracks. It had to be some sort of tactic they taught in cop school... or whatever they call it.

Another knock came at the door, and it was good timing for Sheriff Spencer, because I could've waited him out all night.

The deputy was back. "Sheriff, the groundskeeper from the Honey Springs Country Club called. He said there's been some suspicious activity on the golf course and wanted to know if you could come by to take a look and file a report."

Spencer looked at me then back to the deputy. "Yeah, I'm done here." He stood and ran his hand through his hair. He took a couple of steps over towards the door. He stopped shy of passing me. "Stay out of it."

"Just check the times." I wasn't going to do it, but I did. I said, "If you think you want to question Babette, you need to have me present because she's retained me as her lawyer."

Abruptly, he stopped at the door with his back facing me. I watched with anticipation as his shoulders lifted as he sucked in a breath. They fell back down as he exhaled, and he continued walking without acknowledging what I'd said.

"I'll check with the coroner," was all he said.

Pepper was getting all sorts of pats from the girls who worked up front in the sheriff's department. He was all too happy to hang out with them while I was in Spencer's office trying to convince him to investigate the time of death.

"He's such a sweetheart, Roxy," Gloria Dei said. She was always so nice when I came in here. "Now, tell me what you know about this Hillary Canter girl."

"I was going to ask you the same thing." My brows formed a V. "I'm afraid he's pegged Babette as his number one suspect, but that can't be right."

"I know that they found a photo of a cake in the pocket of that jacket." She had a file sitting on her desk. "And I just filed this," she said. She slid it across her desk to me. "Maybe Hillary had more than one enemy."

"Emily." I looked at the paper knowing I was right that she was a suspect.

"And who else?" she asked, pushing another piece of paper in front of me.

"Pam?" My brows knitted together. Everything I'd been thinking about Pam and how she had a clear motive and very public altercations with Hillary the day before the murder was swirling around in my head.

Gloria shrugged with her lips pinched together.

"He's on his way to her place after he goes to the country club." Gloria took the copy of the warrant to put it back in the file.

"Thanks." I tapped her desk with my fingertips. "Let's go, Pepper. We've got a few things to get cleared up."

Pepper sat in the front seat of my little car. He was so cute. He always sat on his bottom and didn't mind the doggie seat belt I'd bought at A Walk in the Bark. He looked out the windshield like a little person. Even the cows and the running horses along the Kentucky Fence Post didn't make Pepper try and jump up to bark.

"How about some fresh air?" I asked Pepper, rolling down his window. He was able to rest his chin on the door and take in some great country air. "I know I could use some."

The late-day sun was quickly going down. There were more shadows on the pavement from the sun trying to shine through the leaves on the trees, and the air was a little nippy. It was a great refresher for my mind, which was gathering questions for Jean Hill.

There was a fork in the road after the third hairpin curve. I'll never forget the directions Jean's late husband had given me the first time I'd gone to their farm. "At the fork in the road remember the tine is the right time," he'd said. It made no sense whatsoever, but made perfect sense at the same time. The tine meant the fork in the road, and right was the direction.

I veered right at the fork. Not too far ahead was the old, weathered barn wood sign that said Hill's Orchard in bright-red letters. I turned into the driveway.

I was happy to see that the apple trees were still on the right and the grapevines were on the left as far as the eye could see, because I wasn't sure if Jean wanted to keep the orchard going. It was a lot of work.

"Are you ready?" I asked Pepper then unhooked his seat belt. He jumped to his feet and wagged his little stumpy tail. He'd even let out a few howls of delight.

"Is that you, Roxy?" I heard Jean call from the front porch. I could tell there was something in the big ceramic crock sitting in her lap.

"Hi, there," I called. I waved over top the roof of my car and grabbed the bag of scones I thought I would take home. It was always good Southern manners to take something when showing up somewhere unannounced.

Pepper darted out my door and ran up the steps, stopping right next to Jean.

"Oh, Pepper." She giggled. Her fingers were red, and she let him lick them. "He's as delightful as you are." The wrinkles around her eyes deepened. "What's my pleasure?"

"Actually"—I looked into the crock—"I'm here to get some fruit and some questions answered."

"You can have all the fruit you want." She winked. "And you're here on a great day. I've been canning my jams."

"That's what that is." I looked into the crock of what was once rasp-berries. Instead of using a tool to mash them, she used her fingers.

"Come on in." She stood up with the crock situated under one arm. "Can you get the door?"

I hurried around her and grabbed the handle of the old screen door, which let out a welcoming screech when I pulled it open.

"How's everything going?" I asked as I followed her into her old, sixties-style ranch house. I was a little taken aback when I noticed the orange carpet and old apple wallpaper hadn't been replaced.

"Fair to middlin'," she said. She walked over to the jars of jam sitting on the old, wooden kitchen table. "The orchard and farm are doing good. I'm paying the bills. Have a seat."

I did what she said and put the bag of scones on the table. She walked over to the stove and turned the gas knob to light it. She dragged the old steel kettle off the burner and took it to the kitchen sink to fill it up.

"You've got time for a quick cup of coffee?" She returned the kettle to meet the flames. "Now what was it you wanted to ask me?" She grabbed two saucers and cups out of the cabinet.

"I wanted to know about Emily Rich and her working for you." I opened the bag of scones and put one on each saucer Jean had sat down on the table. Emily said she was here and if she was, Jean could be her alibi. "I feel a little responsible for her business going under since I'm the one who talked her into opening it."

"Honey, you can't run the bank." Jean dragged the butter plate that sat out on her table over to her and swiped her scone in it. It was a Southern thing that we all did.

"If her business was doing well, then she wouldn't be late on her payments." I sighed and took a bite of the scone.

The kettle wobbled and wheezed to life. Pepper yelped at the stove and bounced on his paws to see what was making all the ruckus.

Jean and I laughed at him.

Jean made some instant coffee in the cups then brought them over to the table. "The bank called in the full loan. Banks just don't do that out of nowhere. Something down there ain't right."

I looked at her with a critical eye. "I'm sure her dad would've stopped it if that was the case. He is the loan officer."

"All I know is that she needed some quick cash to get the orders filled that she already had, and then she was going to shut down. She owed me money for the fresh milk, cream, and eggs. I told her not to worry about it, but she insisted on paying me back." Jean's hand shook as she brought the cup up to her lips.

"She's working here to do that?" I wanted to be perfectly clear on what I'd understood to be the case.

"That's right," Jean nodded. "She comes here around three a.m. and milks the cows and goats and retrieves the eggs. I even asked her to become full time when she closes the bakery down. Even offered to have her bake her goods here in my home and sell them at the Farmer's Market. Her goods would sell well."

"Yes. They would," I agreed.

I was proof, as someone who went to the Farmer's Market every week and would buy Emily's pastries.

"Was she here at three a.m.?" I asked.

"Sheriff asked me the same question a few minutes ago." Her eyebrows dipped as she frowned.

"Spencer called you?" I asked, wondering how he had the time to get in touch with Jean.

"It was one of the deputies down there," she said. "Is she in some kind of trouble?"

"I sure hope not." I stuffed my face with the rest of my scone. "I sure hope not," I repeated.

CHAPTER ELEVEN

*a*s each hour passed, summer was getting closer, and the morning proved it. Though the sun wasn't out when Pepper and I had gotten to the shop, the air was warm and felt so good going through me on our four a.m. bike ride to the Bean Hive.

I could barely get to sleep the night before after I'd made a list of all the things I needed to do today. The list probably should've been about coffee brewing and baking, but instead it was of places I needed to go.

It just didn't make sense that Emily, Pam, or Babette were suspects. There was no denying that all three wanted to get some sort of justice on Hillary—but murder? That was a far-fetched idea for me, and I was going to prove it. Emily had a clear alibi so I knew she didn't do it, but I was curious about her other fiasco with the bank.

Even Patrick and I cut our conversation short the night before. He was tired from something he had going on at work, and I was tired from thinking about how I was going to help my friends. So we could actually carve out some time together, we made a date for tonight at The Watershed, a fun, upscale restaurant that was located at the end of the boardwalk, opposite the side of the boat dock. Every table had a spectacular view of the lake. It was a white-tablecloth-style restaurant that made for a truly magical date night. It was something to look

89

forward to, and I couldn't wait to tell him about the murder case, even though he wasn't going to like the fact that I was sticking a toe in it.

The morning ritual at the coffeehouse had gone pretty smoothly. I even had time to call Aunt Maxi to see what was going on with her secret investigation. I would've left her a voicemail on her cell phone if it hadn't been full.

The coffee pots had finished brewing. The chicken-and-waffles skillets were already baked and ready for customers. I grabbed the phone and dialed into the shop's messaging system. With the phone to my ear, I headed to the door to flip the sign to OPEN. It was seven a.m. on the dot.

"Roxy, it's Camey." Her voice sounded scared. "I'm in a pickle. Can you please bring me any sort of pastries you have? I'll pay double. Emily called me told me that she couldn't make the hospitality sweets anymore… And we have a contract. What am I going to do? Sue her?" There was a pause. "Call me." The message ended.

I hugged the phone to my chest and tried to calm myself, taking deep breaths while trying to figure out what to do.

"We are just going to have to get what we've got," I said to Pepper on my way back to the kitchen. I dialed Bunny's number, and she answered in a groggy voice. "Bunny, can you come in early?" I asked.

"How early?" she asked.

"Now." I opened the freezer door and started to take out Santa Kisses from Christmas, apple crisp cookies and a few more. Even frozen, they were still good to thaw.

"As in right now?" she questioned.

"Yes. Long story, and I'll tell you when you get here." I knew that would pique her interest.

"I'm getting ready now." She clicked off the phone.

"Of course, she is." I looked down at Pepper. The peanut butter dog treats were on a shelf at his eye level. "Okay. I'll bake some."

Pepper followed on my heels as I carried the loot to the counter and turned down the temperature on the stove. The casseroles were baked at a higher temperature than the sweets. I didn't have time to test and try them. This was a dire situation for Camey.

I called my friend. "Camey?"

"Roxy, you got my message. Can you help me?" She barely took a breath between words.

"I can. Send Walker up in about thirty minutes, and be sure he can take the coffee carafes and bring my other ones back so we can refill them again," I said over her whispered "thank you."

"You're a doll, Roxy." There was more relief in her voice from even a couple of seconds before.

"What did Emily say?" I asked because I'd planned to go see her dad today at the bank to really put my thumb on what was going on.

"She said that the bank had called in her loan, and to kick the poor girl while she was down, the sheriff raided her shop. Hold on." Her voice was muffled, but I could tell she was telling Walker that he needed to come to the shop to get the goods. "Listen, room five has a leak in their bathroom. I've got to go. I'm sending Walker."

She hung up the phone, and I got my cookie sheets out and really greased them up before I got some of the frozen sweets in the oven.

"Good morning," Aunt Maxi trilled when she pushed through the kitchen door. "Roxy, honey, you've got customers."

"I do?" I felt like a deer in headlights.

"You do. You serve customers here." She looked down her nose at me and, picking the fingertip of each of her fingers, plucked her gloves off and tossed them in her purse.

"Gloves?" I asked, quickly popping more cookies and scones in the oven. I pushed the timer on my watch and motioned for her to follow me out to the shop.

"I've got to make some very big decisions today on this thing I'm looking into." She still wasn't going to tell me what the thing was about. "I see where you called me last night." She helped herself to whatever she wanted to eat, and I was perfectly happy with that because while she was back behind the counter, she waited on customers, too.

"You need to delete your old messages," I told her as I made a few more industrial thermoses to have ready for Walker.

"How do you do that?" she asked.

"Are you telling me that you don't get your messages?" I scooped big scoops of my freshly ground summer blend into the big filters. "I don't know why I'm so surprised to find this out."

"Roxanne Bloom, don't you talk out of school." She handed some change back to the customer she was helping. "Come back and see us," she told them then retrieved her phone from her big pocketbook.

She fiddled with it until I finished making the coffee and clicked the pots' switches on.

"Here." I took the phone and swiped my finger left, right and sideways to get to her phone messages. I handed the phone to her. "Now, you click on the ones you want to hear," I said just as the timer on my watch went off. "Delete the ones you don't."

The kitchen was warming and filling with hints of apple and cinnamon as well as some peanut butter.

"Delicious." I was pleased to see the nice tan skin on the cookies. I couldn't help but pick up one of the warm apple crisp cookies and pop the hot sucker in my mouth. "Mmm, that's good."

"Roxy!" Aunt Maxi scared me to death.

"What? They're my cookies." I felt like a scolded child after she'd caught my hand in the cookie jar.

"No." She hurried over to me with the phone stuck out in front of her. "You aren't going to believe who called me."

"Who?" I asked and took the phone from her.

"Hit the last message," she demanded. I was smart enough to know that when Aunt Maxi's voice sounded that way, I knew she meant business, and I did it.

"Maxine, this is Hillary Canter. I heard you were the one that I needed to call for an article on the 'Sticky Situation' page in the paper." There was a sound in the background that I couldn't make out very well. "I've got a scoop for you that'll make your mouth water." Then the phone clicked off.

"Play it again." She pointed.

I replayed it.

"The time on that message is three forty-five a.m." She began to shake. "I think I was the last person she called."

There was suddenly a shift in the world that I could feel clear down to my toes.

"What was that sound when she paused midway through?" I asked. Aunt Maxi gulped. "Do you think she was calling you about the wedding?"

"I do. I think she was going to tell her side of the story. The big fight between her and Pam in here yesterday was the talk of the town."

"It was?" No wonder Spencer had dragged her and Emily into the department. "I think you need to give this information to Spencer. It totally gives Emily an alibi. Now, I just need to find out where Babette was that night."

"She didn't tell you?" Aunt Maxi asked as if I was Babette's keeper.

"I didn't ask." My eyes scanned the coffeehouse. "Yet."

* * *

Pepper jumped up on my leg, bringing out of my thoughts. Ever since Aunt Maxi left, I couldn't stop thinking about the voicemail and the sound that was in the background. At first, the sound was just a strange sound. Given the circumstances, Aunt Maxi and I listened a few more times, and the sound started to take on the sounds of hiccups. It was weird, and I chalked it up to having a very active imagination.

"Do you need to go outside?" I asked Pepper.

The word alone excited the pup into a frenzy. He did circles, yelped, and jumped a few times until I got the leash from the hook.

"Do you think you've got this covered?" I asked Bunny as I bent down to clip the leash on Pepper. A good walk down the pier was what he and I both needed, but for very different reasons.

"Lord have mercy, Roxy. You know I'm good." She said with a voice thick with sarcasm. "You're gonna go look around, aren't you?"

"You never know. It's a good opportunity to go take Pepper on a walk and maybe stop by to see Big Bib." My cell phone rang, and I scurried outside to answer it when I saw it was Mama. "Hey, how's your client?"

"That's what I was calling about." She paused as if she were struggling to find the right words. "It's. . . I don't want to talk over the phone. What if I meet you for lunch at the Bean Hive?"

"That's fine. I'm always there," I said as I noticed out of the corner of my eye that Spencer was walking out of All About the Details and toward me. "Come, Pepper," I whispered and tugged on the leash for us to walk the other way.

"You're walking Pepper?" Mama asked.

"Roxy!" Spencer yelled. "Roxanne!"

"Who's that?" Mama asked, sounding a bit confused.

"It's Spencer, and I was hoping he didn't see me," I grumbled and stopped after he yelled my name again, adding that he knew I saw him. "I'll see you at lunch."

I clicked off the phone and turned around, practically running into him.

"Why didn't you stop when I called you name?" His features hardened. "I know you heard me because you suddenly acted like one of those crazy speed-walking people in the mall."

"I was on the phone with my mom." I took a few steps over to where Pepper was smelling a plank. "What's going on with Hillary's murder?"

"We found a photo of a cake that Emily Rich had designed. I heard Hillary hadn't been so nice about Emily baking the wedding cake." He divulged more information than he normally did, which put me on alert. "Did you know that Emily was having money issues?"

"Are you asking me for your investigation?" I pushed a strand of my curls behind my ear.

"What if I was?" he asked. "Not that you have any business whatsoever looking into this, but you do play the lawyering-up card a lot. I figured we might as well work as a team. People talk to you more than they talk to me."

"Go on," I encouraged him.

I wasn't going to lie. It felt good that he finally seemed to be listening to me about how coffee and a little sweet treat make people feel comfortable. That level of what I liked to call "the feels" was when people started to talk. There was a lot of gossip going around the coffeehouse about Hillary and her family's finances.

"I'm not asking you to go undercover and put yourself in danger." His voice was tight as he spoke. "I'm just asking you to call me if you hear anything strange."

"For starters, I think Hillary's last call on her cell phone was to Aunt Maxi." We walked past Walk in The Bark. Pepper tried to tug us across the boardwalk to get inside. He knew that Morgan Keys, the owner, would give him not only some good scratches, but a few treats. "On our way back," I promised him. I had to fight him the entire way past Touched by an Angel Spa and The Crooked Cat Book Shop.

"We couldn't find her cell phone." His words sent chills to my bones. "Her parents signed a release of records since they paid for it, and Gloria sent in the warrant. We should have them back by the end of today. Why do you think she called Maxine?" he asked. We walked down the ramp toward the parking lot of The Watershed.

There was a nice grassy area along the shoreline where Pepper loved to run and smell. It was good for us to go here a couple of times a day so he wasn't so cooped up in the coffeehouse.

"She left a message after three thirty a.m., which means that Emily Rich was in no way involved in killing Hillary because she was at Jean Hill's orchard milking the cows and goats and whatever else could be milked so she could pay off some debts."

I bent down and unclipped Pepper's leash. While I did that, Spencer pulled out his little notebook and scribbled away.

"Yeah, we released her last night after we checked her alibi. I did call the coroner, and he said Hillary took her last breath around four a.m." He sucked in a deep breath and gazed out over the lake. "Pam doesn't have an alibi. The evidence is piling up against her more and more, with the arguments and the fact that Hillary was going to pay off the rest of the wedding."

It took a lot for me to not say "I told you so," but we were all adults, and I was kind of digging the fact that he wanted my expertise, advice, and help.

"Hillary was a hard one to take. She even knocked my coffee shop down." I held my hand up over my brow to shield the bright sun so I could watch Pepper play in the shallow edge of the water. "I'd heard her family was having financial problems, which I found odd since she was going to pay for the wedding."

"You did?" His brows furrowed. His eyes shifted left to right a couple of times before he clamped his mouth shut and flipped through his little notebook. He dragged his finger down the page and said, "I interviewed her parents, and they didn't mention it."

"Maybe it's not true. Again, I hear a lot of gossip, and though it's just lips flapping, I've always found that there was some truth in there somewhere. You just have to weed it out."

"Mr. Canter was full of himself. He can strut while sitting down."

I laughed.

"Seriously, all joking aside, what about your friend Babette? I keep asking her to help me, but she keeps saying the she had nothing to do with it. She was at home, where she lives alone, so no one can prove it. Her coat was on the victim, though she claims she left it at her shop, and Jana said that Hillary and Babette had that big blow up."

"Hillary said she had a big scoop for Aunt Maxi's gossip column, which makes me think it was about Pam or Babette." A pontoon boat was motoring down the lake towards the boat dock, which made me remember that I wanted to talk to Big Bib about the incident with Babette and his girlfriend years ago.

"Why was she on the boardwalk at three thirty a.m.? Who was she meeting? What did she want to tell Maxi?" He asked all the questions I'd been asking myself. "I asked her father why he thought she was on the boardwalk so early in the morning, and he said that he never kept tabs on her. She was a grown woman."

"Aunt Maxi said she was going to come down and let you listen to the message." I remembered the funny sound in the middle of it. "There's something I can't make out in the voicemail. Hillary didn't sound distressed, and in the middle of her message, there was a hiccup sound in the background or something." I shrugged. "I keep telling myself it was my imagination getting the best of me, since I really want to find this killer." I clamped my lips together.

"No, no." Spencer waged his finger at me. "You will not find a killer. I said 'gossip.' I want you to listen to the gossip in the safety of your coffee shop." He gave me a stern look. "Got it?"

"Got it." I saluted him. "Pepper! Let's go!"

Before Spencer left, he confirmed Aunt Maxi's cell phone number. He was planning to call her, but I knew he would get the voicemail-was-full message.

On our way back down the boardwalk, Pepper wasn't about to let me pass up seeing Morgan. His leash was a long, retractable one, and he had it extended and taut to the fullest before I'd even made it to the edge of the Crooked Cat Book Shop.

Morgan greeted us with her bright smile. "Someone was scratching on my door, and I wondered if it was you," she said to Pepper. Her brown hair looked pretty as if fell down over her fair skin. "Can he?" she asked before she gave him a treat.

"He'd be mad if you didn't." It gave me joy to see how happy Pepper made people. He was so sweet and gentle.

"Come on in." She didn't even have to say it because Pepper had already run into her shop and sat next to the counter where she kept the treat jar.

"Just for a minute. I've got to get back," I said, walking inside the door to wait for Pepper to grab his treat. "Did you change things around?" I asked.

"Yes. I try to do that every year before the big tourist season comes. More and more people are bringing their animals to the lake, so I decided to make a whole section of dog life vests and goggles." She walked over and held up a life vest with four armholes. "Aren't they the cutest?"

"This must've taken a long time." I looked at the wall and the three rows of shelves she had dedicated to the boaters' animals to match their aquatic lifestyle.

"It took me all night." She popped the lid off the jar.

The sound alone made Pepper squirm with delight. I couldn't help but smile at how cute he was. His little mustache quivered with anticipation of what she had in her hand when she bent down. She opened her palm, and he gently took it from her and darted off to the back corner where there was a dog bed.

I gasped. "Pepper!"

"He's fine." She waved off my concern.

"His paws are wet from getting into the lake surf." My brows furrowed. "Oh, well. We need another dog bed." My jaw dropped. "Did you say 'all night'?" I asked.

"And for the past couple of days." She sighed.

"Did you hear about Hillary Canter?" I asked.

"No." She shook her head. "What about her?"

"She was murdered on the boardwalk a couple nights ago. Strangled." I watched as her brown eyes grew bigger. "Around three thirty a.m. to be exact. Were you here then?"

"Here? Yeah. I thought I heard something. I looked out the window and didn't see anything. It was strange, too," she said.

"What do you mean, 'strange'?" I asked.

"I swear I heard someone with a bad case of the hiccups." She confirmed that my imagination hadn't taken over when I'd listened to Aunt Maxi's voicemail.

"Do you mind calling Spencer at the sheriff's department and telling him that?" I asked.

"Not at all." She shook her head. "That's awful." Her brows dipped. "I've been so wrapped up in this shop that I haven't even looked at the paper or watched the news." She opened a drawer from the counter and looked through it before she pulled out a calendar. "Tonight is the

Southern Women's Club monthly meeting. Beverly Canter is the president. I wasn't going to go, but I think I will now."

"Tonight?" I asked, wondering if I should go and pretend to be checking out the club.

Aunt Maxi had been trying to get me involved in every club and organization in Honey Springs, though she wasn't a member of this one.

"Yes. Seven thirty." Morgan tapped on the calendar. "I think I'll go."

"Do they let in non-members?" I asked.

"It's your lucky day, Roxy Bloom," she said. She let out a raucous sound of laughter. "We are having a membership drive. I get a gift card for every person I bring."

"Seven thirty, where?" I asked.

"We meet in the gathering space in the library." She and I both looked at the door when a customer came in with a dog. "Meet me there, or I can pick you up."

"I'll meet you there." I knew I needed to talk to Patrick because we'd made plans to go on a date, but I really wanted to go and see what everyone was saying about the Canters and their financial well-being—if any of it was true.

From what I'd heard, there were far more tales twisted at those meetings than learning how to be a good southern woman. But that was just hearsay.

CHAPTER TWELVE

*W*hen Pepper and I passed the Bean Hive on our way down to the boat dock, I could see Bunny holding a meeting with a few of her friends through the windows. The coffee shop looked to be okay. I imagined they were in deep conversation about the murder, and I hoped that Bunny would have some good gossip after I got back from going to see Bib.

All of the shops looked filled and without looking at my watch, I could tell it was almost time for lunch because the smell of fries and burgers floated out of the Buzz In and Out Diner. The tented chalkboard outside of the restaurant even boasted their delicious, meaty beef burger as the special of the day. It also said the beef was provided by the Cattlemen's Association, and that was a big deal in Honey Springs. They had the best and freshest beef around. Almost every Friday night during the summer, they would set up a grilling station in Central Park. It was a standing date for Patrick and me. Plus, it was a great time for members of the community to get together and visit with each other.

My stomach grumbled when another whiff of fries floated past my nose. Pepper must've smelled it too, because he started to veer toward the diner.

"Not today, buddy." I gently held the leash taut.

The boardwalk was getting more crowded, and I could see that the parking lot was filled with trucks that were either pulling a boat or had an empty boat trailer. The buzz of revving boat engines sounded all over the marina, followed by billows of exhaust smoke.

The marina had a typical boat shop, which was more of a general store for boaters but with one difference. It was a floating, cottage-style shop that fit in with the rest of the cute shops on the boardwalk. The beautification committee had taken extra steps with the renovation of the boardwalk to make sure the shops looked cozy and made the board-walk feel as though it was its own small town within a small town.

"Big Bib?" I called, feeling a little odd that I still called him by his nickname. "It's Roxy and Pepper."

I looked around to see if I could see him and checked out all the essentials he sold, such as fire extinguishers, life jackets, floats, fishing equipment, boat batteries, beer, snacks, coolers, koozies, and much more.

It appeared that he was also gearing up for the summer tourists because his snack items were fully stocked, the mini-grills were stacked on top of each other, and there were coolers galore. I didn't know what it was, but there was a connection between being on the water and needing lots of food.

Patrick fell into the needing-food-on-the-water category. Every time we went to the lake for an afternoon of fishing or just a ride around, he made sure he packed a light cooler of food and drinks. The cooler was the first thing he popped open before we even dropped a line.

Pepper darted around the shop, smelling anything he could get his sniffer on while I looked for Bib. He was usually behind the cash register, watching the TV.

"Where are you," I whispered to myself and glossed over the shelves to see if he was bent over.

Not that you could miss him. He was a big, burly man who always had on a pair of jeans, a Metallica shirt that he'd cut the sleeves off of, and a pair of red suspenders clipped onto the waistband of his jeans. It was his staple outfit no matter what season it was. Sometimes the shirt changed to a different heavy metal band, but that was rare.

Pepper lifted his paw and scratched at the glass door that was opposite the door we came in. That door led straight out to the marina piers that jutted out into Lake Honey Springs and had the boat slips attached.

I opened the door for Pepper to run around and sniff. I stepped outside to see if I could find Bib working on a boat. The warmth of the sun reflecting off the metal covering of the boat slips put a pleasant welcome on my cheeks. It'd been a bitter winter with lots of snow and a long, chilly spring that made me deeply desire the coming of summer.

I closed my eyes and tuned into my breath for about a second before I heard an engine rumble to a stop and Bib's voice over top of it.

"I'm tired of waiting around. How old do we have to be to enjoy ourselves?" he asked whoever he was talking to. Then, a curse fell from his mouth.

I was sure he made the devil blush with his words.

"I do love you." The returned voice left me stunned because I knew it was Babette. "I just don't think the looming of Hillary Canter's murder and me as the suspect looks good."

I tiptoed a couple of paces toward their voices and peered around one of the metal beams that held a metal roof overtop the slips.

"You can solve this mess with the sheriff if you come clean. Don't you understand that you could go to jail for a crime you didn't commit?" he asked with unbridled anger in his voice. "You were with me. That's your alibi, and it gets you off the hook." Bib choked with fury.

I peeked around a little more and saw how he glowered at her, which forced her to turn away. Then, I quickly remembered that hiding and sneaking around was never my strong suit when Babette's face flushed white as she saw me.

"Roxy?" she gasped and appeared to shiver in panic. "Are you spying on us?"

"I.. um..." I stepped out from behind my hiding post and walked towards them. "I didn't mean to overhear. I was out here looking for

Bib to ask him some questions about you and your past, since he was part of it." I blinked a few times. "It's all because you asked me to look into this as your lawyer. I don't understand that you didn't tell me you were with Bib the night of Hillary's murder."

"Because I'm taking my chances on you clearing me. This isn't how I wanted the world to find out that years after the accident with Paige, I finally bagged the prize," she spat with anger that brought tears to her eyes. "Even though you've not lived in Honey Springs long, you know that they hear a rumor or find out that we are an item, and I'll be tried and hung all over again for the terrible accident that happened so many years ago."

"You did your time. You paid the price for that. Everyone who loves you wants you to be happy. And if it's with Bib, and it can clear your names with Spencer, then I think this is a great time to tell the world that you've found love." I pointed to Bib. "But I thought you were an item with Leslie Roarke?"

Leslie Roarke owned the Crooked Cat Bookstore. Just a few months ago, she and Bib seemed to be hot and heavy at the Moose Lodge and in public.

"Nah, Leslie is a good friend." He shook that notion off real fast.

I glanced over at Babette. By the look on her face, I could tell that panic was rioting within her. The movement of her jaw, the fidgeting eyes, and the biting back of tears were just a few of the movements I could see. I could only imagine what was going through her head.

"Roxy is right. She's a lawyer, for goodness sake." Bib threw up his hands. "I'm telling you that when I get done with this boat, if you've not gone to the sheriff's department to tell him that you were with me, then I will." He shook his head. "You can dump me or whatever is going on in that head of yours, but that's the chance I'm taking so you don't go to jail again."

"Losing you would shatter me." Her eyes anxiously searched his face.

"You know that I've been wanting to come clean for years about us. This is the time, or you will lose me." There didn't seem to be any room for negotiation in his voice.

"As your lawyer"—I did love using that when I had my practice—"I can't ethically let you do this to yourself just because you think you'll be in the next installment of the 'Sticky Situation.'" I gave her a half-smile. "Trust me when I say that this might go around the gossip mill a few times in a twenty-four-hour period." I circled my finger between them. "But something new and better will come along right after that, and your news will be old news."

"You do know how all this gossip works around here." She swallowed with difficulty and suddenly found her voice as she turned to Bib. "You and I are meant to be together. I did pay for my mistake years ago, and it's time to let that go. Roxy, will you go with me to see Spencer?"

"Yes." I nodded my head. "Right now?" I asked.

"Might as well get it over with." Her words ran together, and before she could get them out, Bib grabbed her and swung her around.

"Yeehaw!" he hollered with delight. "Finally." He planted a big ol' Bib kiss on her lips. "I love this woman!" he yelled across the boat dock.

"Good, now get over here and get my boat going," someone chirped back.

He held her tightly. "Baby, we're going to celebrate tonight."

"The Watershed has to be full on reservations," she said.

"You want to go to The Watershed?" I asked, and they nodded. "I'll make it happen."

I knew that when I told Patrick about my change in plans, he wouldn't be happy. If I told him that we could give our reservations to Bib and Babette, I might just be able to give him a smile.

CHAPTER THIRTEEN

"You're telling me that you and Bib have been an item for the past couple of months?" Spencer asked from across the cold, metal table in the interrogation room.

When we first got there, he tried to say that I had to stay out of the room, but I played the lawyer card and said that Babette wasn't going to be interviewed without me being there.

"Yes"—her voice was low—"when we started to work on the Annual Honey Festival. It was a bit uncomfortable because we really never talked about what happened years ago." She was barely audible. The microphone made a loud noise across the metal as Spencer slid it closer to her mouth. "We were on the decorating committee together this year, and since all the decorations for the festival are kept in my shop, he was strong enough to move them around for us. We spent a lot of time getting the festival decorations up all over town, and I got to know him all over again as the man he's become, and he saw the changes in me since we were in high school."

"He can vouch for you under oath?" Spencer asked.

He seemed to be letting her off easy, and that sent my intuition into a flutter. I wondered what he was doing.

"You wait here, and I'll get you a sheet of paper and a pen so you can write it all down and sign it. Then, we can legally get you off the list." He stood up and scooted his chair back.

Babette nodded. I stood up and held my hand out for her to stay, following him out.

"Listen." I stopped him after shutting the door behind me. "You're letting her off way too easy in there. And if you want my help, I need to know what you're thinking."

"I only asked you to keep your ear to the ground at your coffee-house for any information. Not actively go out and interrogate people." His stare drew down his nose and rested on my eyes. "Besides, I'm a bit surprised after our conversation today that you didn't tell me about the little episode between Hillary and Pam at the Bean Hive. I had a very interesting conversation with Loretta Bebe today when she came in here out of the goodness and conscientious-ness of her heart."

For one thing, Loretta didn't have a heart or a conscience. Spencer was baiting me, and I knew I should've told him, but I thought I had time to question Pam. It was the bombshell that Bib was Babette's alibi that blew up my plan to go see Pam.

"It's Pam," I shot back. You're going after Pam. How did Pam get the coat out of All About the Details?"

"I have enough evidence to make an arrest," he confirmed. "Think about it. You girls dream of what your wedding is going to look like as soon as you leave the womb."

"Not all, but most." I wanted to clarify.

"Go with me here." The suggestion of annoyance hovered in his eyes. "Pam has this big notebook that I seized from Babette. It dates back years. In her head, this was what she wanted. In comes her best friend Hillary who feeds her these ideas, and the money is adding up. Hillary tells her not to worry because she will pay for the wedding. What are rich best friends for?"

"Then, you think that Pam bought into all that? But, good girl that Pam is, she got sick of how Hillary treated the people around her and took over the wedding?" I asked.

"I also went to see Truman." I detected a thawing in his voice. "It appears that Hillary made a pass at him and Pam walked in on it."

I gasped. "Oh my."

"Even though Pam says she didn't kill Hillary, there's no one that can give her an alibi. She claims that she was at home asleep. There's no video footage from any of the shops." He didn't say it, but I was getting the feeling that he was still mad that I didn't tell him about the fight.

My phone chirped from my back pocket.

"I'm going to get her the paperwork so I can get her out of here." He walked away shaking his head. "Can't believe Bib and Babette are an item."

"Mama!" I answered my phone with a gasp when I realized I'd forgotten about our lunch date. "I'm so sorry. Are you at the Bean Hive?"

"Yes, and I don't have time to wait. I have to go to the office." She sounded flustered. "I'll just have to talk to you later."

"I'm actually going to be going to the bank in a few." I still had to get some things done on my list, and heading to the bank to talk to Evan Rich was on the top. I just couldn't shake the pickle Emily and the Bee's Knees Bakery was in without feeling guilty. "What if I swing by then?"

"Sounds great. Bye, honey." She hung up.

While I waited for Babette to sign the papers, I sent Patrick a text. Although I wanted to believe that I decided to text him because I was taking Timmy's schedule into consideration and didn't want to disrupt their time together, I couldn't say that. The fact was that I didn't want to hear Patrick groan and moan when I told him I couldn't go to supper. I needed to try to convince him to let Babette and Big Bib have the reservation at the restaurant.

Like a coward, I texted him that we needed to reschedule and a quick sentence about giving it to Bib and Babette. A little bubble appeared under my text, and a "text read" message popped up under my message. He didn't respond. My heart hurt because I knew he was upset, but maybe I could stop by his house after I went to the bank and stopped by to see Mama.

I sucked in a deep breath and let out a long sigh. The feeling of being stretched thin was starting to wear on me. I'd not had this feeling since I was in law school studying for the Bar Exam.

Spencer popped his head out of the room. "Roxy, Babette said that you can go on and go. Bib is going to come get her. Something about a table coming available at the Watershed or something."

"Great." I smiled knowing that Patrick's kind heart did extend to the couple.

Not dropping Babette off would save me some time, and if I played my cards right, I could fit in all the errands I needed to run. First, I needed to stop by the Bean Hive to pick up a few treats. I never liked to go anywhere empty handed.

"Everyone thinks it's Pam that killed Hillary." Bunny and everyone else took the easy road to pointing fingers. "I don't blame her. There were also some rumblings about the bank calling in a lot of people's loans. What on earth is going on? Honey Springs is going to hell in a handbasket." Bunny eased down on one of the stools.

The bell over the door dinged, and the two afternoon girls came in looking so cute in their ponytails and Bean Hive tees.

"I'm so glad they're here. I'm worn slap out." Bunny untied the apron from around her girth and slapped it on top of the counter.

"Did you hear whose loans?" I asked.

"Nah, they didn't know. Just some rumblings. You know how all them old women can be." Her words made me giggle.

Yes, I knew how they could be, and Bunny was one of them.

"You go on and get home. I'm gonna grab a few mini-quiches to drop off while I run some errands." I gave her a quick hug before I headed back into the kitchen. I made sure I cooked plenty of things and put them in the freezer for times like this. When I showed up to someone's house or place of business, I loved to take a treat to break any sort of ice. It was just a nice gesture that worked.

Going to see Mama was first on my list. I felt bad enough that she'd moved around her schedule to come see me at the boardwalk. It must've been something pretty important because since she got her real estate licenses, she's been busy and working very hard, leaving little time during the day to visit.

With Pepper tucked in the basket, my messenger bag strapped across my body, and the treats carefully stowed inside, we were on our way. It was a seven-minute bike ride to town.

Downtown hadn't changed much since I visited as a teenager. The hubbub of most activities and festivals that took place in Honey Springs were held in Central Park, which was smack-dab in the middle of town.

Central Park was surrounded by a very nice walking or jogging path. The sidewalks also extended into the park and led up to a big white gazebo. When I passed it, I couldn't help but think about Pam and her wedding. Originally, she wanted it to be in Central Park, perched inside with Truman like those porcelain bride-and-groom figurines on top of a wedding cake.

It would have been very picturesque. What was left of the various colored daffodils that popped out around the park because entwined with red-and-white roses and the Kentucky wild flowers that bloomed with vibrancy this time of the year.

I jerked my eyes away after I'd pictured Patrick and me standing up there. I was a little surprised at my own imagination, since I'd yet to think about what the wedding would look like. It was one of those things where I'd already been there and done that, so I didn't see the hurry. It didn't mean I wasn't completely head over heels in love with Patrick. Oh, I was. I'd loved him since the day I saw him hammering away at Aunt Maxi's when we were children. It was hard to explain, and I wasn't sure I was going to be able to hold him off much longer without setting a date.

I put that in the back of my head and noticed the banners hanging from the carriage lights that dotted downtown had the banners had been switched out to the Lake Honey Springs logo with the boat and lake. The beautification committee took great pride in switching those out for the festivals and the seasons. It was just another added touch that made Honey Springs a very cozy small town that we all loved.

The first building on Main Street was the Honey Springs Church. I couldn't stop the memories of how Patrick and me used to slip out the back door before Sunday school would start. We weren't doing anything bad, just acting like two teenagers who like to spend time down on the shore of Lake Honey Springs. Aunt Maxi said that if I didn't watch it, I was gonna lose my religion on that lake. I didn't know what she meant at the time.

Next to church was the firehouse and sheriff's department, where I'd gone to see Shepard earlier. Across the street from that was the Moose Lodge. All of these were right before the big circle in the middle, which was Central Park.

Along Main Street were the Brandt's Fill 'er Up, Klessinger Realty, where Mama's office was, the courthouse and city hall, Donald's Barber Shop, a medical building, and the local community college, which was where the library was located.

It turned out to be a beautiful day for a late-afternoon bike ride, and the fresh air did me some good.

"Hi, Ursula," I greeted the secretary that Mama and the other realtors used. She sat at the desk with her cat-eye glasses pushed clear up on the bridge of her nose. Her beady green eyes seemed to snap at me. Her hair was pinned to her head in close curls. She looked as if she was stuck in the fifties and should be home in the kitchen making a pot roast for supper.

"Roxy." She appeared to have forced her lips into a tight smile. "Penny is in the courtyard."

"Good." I set the Bean Hive to-go bag on her desk. "That means you can eat these all by yourself."

"Quiche?" Ursula's smile turned into a genuine grin.

"Bacon and spinach. Your favorite." I clearly remembered how Mama had taken some of my extra quiche to the office then telling me that Ursula had loved them.

"You are a dear." Her shoulders lifted to her ears in delight.

I left another satisfied customer—who was very hard to please—happy and smiling as I made my way down the hall towards the back door. Each of the businesses had its own fenced-in courtyard. Some were fancier than others, but the real estate offices had a retractable awning on the back as well as some nice patio furniture. They liked to work outside when they could, even hosting events once a month with customers who had purchased a house in that month.

I looked out the window of the door before I pushed it open. Mama was pacing in the far-right corner of the fence. Her lips were moving a mile a minute, and she continued to put her fingers in her mouth. No doubt she was chewing on her nails because that's what she did when she was stressed.

"Hey, Mama," I called. Her head jerked up. She waved me over. "Are you okay?" I asked as I handed her a bag of mini-quiche. "I'd like to say these might help, but you look frazzled."

"Is that what you call it?" She chewed on the edge of her lip. "I'm more than frazzled. I'm just... just..." She shook her head and put her finger back in her mouth.

"Stop that." I tried to pull her arm down. "What's wrong?"

She stopped pacing in front of me and looked around, twisting her body to look over the privacy fence around the courtyard.

"You aren't going to believe it"—she looked me square in the eye—"Someone over at the bank is slicker than a boiled onion." She tugged me closer. She whispered, "My client. The one I was telling you about."

"Yes," I replied.

"Well, I told you she was moving, and she needed to sell her house. It's a cute house. Little." She waved her hand around. "Maybe one hundred and ten thousand dollars at the most. And it's behind the courthouse. Not even on Lake Honey Springs or nothing. Well"—there was a glint of worry in Mama's eyes—"she hired me to sell it, only she ain't got a clear deed."

"You mean she has a second mortgage?" I asked.

"That she didn't take out. When I called the mortgage company, they told me that they haven't gotten the payoff for the house. I told them that I sold it about nine months ago. Plenty of time to get the check from the closing company to them."

"Mama, that's impossible." I knew as a lawyer that these things rarely happened.

"No, it's not. There was a lien put on the house from Cane Contractors. When I called Patrick about it, he wouldn't talk to me." Her words shocked me.

"He's not said a word to me." I wondered if that was what all the meetings he'd been going to were about. He'd seemed very preoccupied-—not that a house of that size would put his company under.

"The loan company won't help me, either. They said they'd get back to me. In the meantime, I've got an upset client. And I think something fishy went on with the bank." The lines between her eyes deepened.

"What can I do?" I asked, knowing this was what she wanted me to look into.

"I want you to use them God-given brains and the money I paid to get you through law school to get this mess straightened out." She pointed to her chest. "I've got a bad feeling about this."

"I'm sure it's just a mix-up." I was sure of it. "Maybe an oversight in paperwork. A check got put into a different account by accident. Something."

As I gave her a voice of reason, she seemed to calm down a little. "And you'll talk to Patrick?" she asked.

"As a matter of fact, I have to go to the bank today to talk to Evan Rich. Poor Emily's business isn't doing so well, and she had to close." My tormented feelings started to creep in. "I feel somewhat responsible, since I practically talked him into letting her open The Bee's Knees Bakery."

"Sometimes young people are just not mature enough. They see money coming in, and they spend it. Maybe she didn't put the profits back into the business."

Mama was right. "That's what I'm afraid of, and I want to help her get out of the business without having debts to pay." I reached out and put my hand on Mama's arm. "While I'm there, I'll see if he can pull up the initial loan for your client."

"That'd be great." Mama took off towards the building. "I need to get you the paperwork with the original loan number and what the bank lending mortgage deed was going to be."

"Sounds good." I followed behind her. "After that, I'm going to run some treats over to Patrick's house. He's babysitting Timmy for Debbie today."

"He's not working?" Mama asked, opening the door to her office.

Mama's cute glass-top desk sat in front of a big window, surrounded by shiplap walls. The built-in bookcases were on one wall, and she had a little snack counter with a mini fridge on the opposite wall. She'd decorated it in a super-cozy style with a big brown leather couch decorated with fuzzy pillows. A brown rug covered the majority of the hardwood floor, and a glass coffee table sat in front of the couch.

"I guess he took the day off because Debbie is in a little bit of a pickle," I said, really wondering what kind of pickle she was in.

"Here you go." Mama handed me the file. "This is a copy. It has my client's name and address—all the information the bank should need to pull up the documents. I'll come by your place later tonight."

"I won't be home. I've got to go to the Southern Women's Club, but I can call you after that," I said.

Ursula wasn't at her desk on my way out, so I jotted down a quick note to leave for her. It said that I hoped she'd enjoyed the quiche, and it was nice to see her. I tried to go that little extra mile to make sure customers were happy. Not that she was a customer today, but she'd come to the coffeehouse before, and I'd found that the little extras were what meant the most to people.

I hopped on my bike and headed the other direction towards the courthouse and past the medical building to where the Honey Springs National Bank was located. It was the most modern structure in Honey Springs, but that wasn't saying much.

No matter where you were in the bank, you could hear what everyone was saying even at a whisper due to the concrete floors and openness of the space. There were two large glass offices on the right and a teller line straight ahead. The office that had a sign that said "loan officer" belonged to Evan Rich, who was Emily's dad and the main reason I was there.

When I noticed he wasn't in the office, I looked into the office next to his with the president's sign on the closed door. Since it too was glass, I could see Evan in there with the man who was the bank's president.

Before I sat down in the fake-leather seat between the offices, I read the name plate on the president's door.

Mr. Canter. I blinked and blinked again.

"Mr. Canter as in Hillary?" I asked myself as I looked into the glass office. I squinted when I noticed some photos on the credenza behind him, but I couldn't make out who was in them.

Quickly, I headed up to the teller's window.

"May I help you?" she asked.

"I never know which color to choose." I fingered the bowl of tiny suckers on the counter. "But I think root beer is always a good choice." I grabbed one with brown barrels on it.

"No one ever picks the root beer." She looked as if she smelled something terrible.

"Lucky me." I plucked the paper off and stuck the round ball of candy in my mouth. "Do you know how long Mr. Rich is going to be?" I asked, letting the sucker stick jerk up and down between my lips. I thought I was playing it casual.

"I'm not sure. I don't know if you know Mr. Canter, but his niece was brutally murdered, and I'm sure he's giving the reins over to Mr. Rich for a couple of weeks. They've been in there all morning." The girl behind the counter sighed.

"Brutally murdered?" I asked.

"Oh, yes. On the boardwalk." Her chin slowly went up then down. "I don't care how much they try to fix up that boardwalk. I told my friends that you never know who comes to Honey Springs during the tourist season. It could've been a serial killer."

"Or a disgruntled bank employee getting back at the president," I suggested, making her draw back in sheer fright.

"Roxy? Is that you?" I heard my name echo through the building.

"Mr. Rich." I tried to stay focused on him on my way over, but I couldn't help but zero in on Mr. Canter, who was standing with his back to the bank, looking out the window. "I wanted to talk to you about Emily and the Bee's Knees."

"Come on in." He shut the door behind me after I walked in. "Right here is probably not the place to talk about it."

"I feel a little responsible since she's just a nineteen-year-old girl. She's an amazing pastry chef, but that doesn't mean she's a good business woman. I really should've continued to mentor her." I found myself looking at him to tell me it was okay. "I understand she wasn't paying her loan. I feel awful. It's about more than the baking or brewing the coffee. There's the business side."

"I'm sorry, Roxy. The truth is that the bank had to call her loan back." He looked down at his hands. "I too may be out of a job because I'm not sure the bank is going to survive itself."

"This bank?" I questioned. My entire life savings was riding on this bank.

"It's in the early stages. But we've over-extended our loans. Though I can't say that it's my fault, since I am the only loan officer here." There were sweat beads on his bald head.

"Does this have to do with mortgages?" Suddenly, the caring-about-his-daughter part of my brain switched to the lawyer side of my brain. "Because one of my mama's clients—" I started to say before I was interrupted.

"Evan, I need you in my office." Mr. Canter didn't bother knocking before he interrupted us. I could definitely see where Hillary had gotten her manners.

"I'm sorry. We'll have to talk later." Mr. Rich jumped up out of his chair and headed toward the door. "Did the trustees call a meeting?"

"Yes. We need to get. . ." was all I heard from Mr. Canter's mouth before he slammed his door shut.

"You know, I thought I recognized you." The teller called me back over. "I've been in your shop after work. You're usually running out the door and the afternoon girls are there, but I do love your specialty brews."

"Thank you." I wished I had more treats with me. "Why don't you come down to the shop after you get off work, and I'll have them give you one for free."

"You'd do that?" she asked.

"Of course, I would. I don't want you to keep thinking the boardwalk is dangerous, because it's really not." I smiled.

"It was your shop where Mr. Canter's niece was found, right?" She asked with wide eyes, which I could tell was a smoke screen.

If she wanted information, I'd give it to her, but I also wanted information. "She was. Do you think it has anything to do with what's going on here?" I asked.

"No." She dragged her chin left to right. "I'd heard they fired that girl from the mortgage company. She was depositing them checks into a personal account."

"You mean she was depositing mortgage-closing checks that were supposed to go to the mortgage company into someone's personal account?" I questioned.

"That's what I assume happened." She looked around and leaned far over the teller counter. "There has to be someone who works at the bank that helped her."

"Huh?" I wasn't following.

"Think about it. How else did she get a check deposited into our bank if she couldn't sign for it? It had to be someone on the inside who let it go through." Her brows rose. "The sheriff's department has been on it all day. Even the newspaper lady came in here." She looked off into the distance. "Strange little old woman."

Without me having to ask, I knew she meant Aunt Maxi. "If I give you a name and some documents, do you think you could check on your little computer to see if her home mortgage has been affected by this recent turn of banking events?"

Her face clouded with uneasiness.

"Listen, I'm her attorney." I was getting really good at this lying stuff.

"She is going to go bankrupt because of this. Can you just put yourself in her shoes for a second?"

Biting her lip, she looked away.

"Please?" I was not below begging.

There was a pensive shimmer in the shadow of her eyes. "Give it to me."

"Great." I pulled the file out of my messenger bag and handed her the document Mama had prepared with the client's information on it for quick reference. "That's her name, social security number, and loan number."

"Mm-hmm." She typed away with her eyes glued to the screen. Awkwardly, she cleared her throat and started to write something on a piece of paper. She slid the paper across the counter. "That's your beginning balance and what you've got as of today in your checking, Ms. Bloom."

I looked down. She'd scribbled that the loan was taken out by the builder of Mama's client's house. The client's check to the mortgage company, Bank Lending Mortgage, was deposited into J.J Builder's bank account.

JJ Builder's was the builder who'd built Mama's client's house. I clearly remember seeing the name in the file.

"Excuse me." Her eyes grazed the top of my shoulder. "Can I help you?" she asked the customer behind me.

"You might want to withdraw your money," I muttered to the customer on my way out. I thought about taking my own advice.

The afternoon was quickly dwindling away. On my bike ride back to the coffeehouse, I couldn't even enjoy the warmth of the fresh breeze because my mind was so jumbled with what might be going on at the bank—or even with the big mortgage company.

When Pepper and I got back to the coffeehouse, the younger school crowd was already there. Not all the dog treats I made had been taken, so I decided to take them to Morgan.

I told the afternoon staff goodnight and handed them the checklist to do before they left—simple things such as refilling all the condiments, cleaning all the tables and floors, and refilling the coffee pots so I just had to flip them on in the morning.

Pepper and I headed down to Walk in The Bark with the fur treats in hand.

"Hi, there," I greeted Morgan when I walked into her shop. "It's getting busy out there."

The boats were trolling in a single-file line in Lake Honey Springs, and the boardwalk had a lot of foot traffic.

"Yes. So many boaters coming early this year." Morgan was using the hand-tagger to tag new pieces of clothing. "I talked to Spencer after you left. I told him what I'd heard, and he took down a statement. I sure hope it helped."

Pepper ran towards her with this tail wagging. She bent down and picked him up to give him some kisses before I clipped his leash back on him.

"Anything, no matter how big or small, will help." My mind wasn't on the murder. It was on the bank. "Do you own your shop or lease it?"

I knew some of the shops were owned either by Cane Contractors and Aunt Maxi, but I wasn't sure about Morgan's.

"I bought it from J.J. Builders when they were doing the renovation a year ago." She continued to work. "Why, do they own the coffeehouse?"

"No. Aunt Maxi owns my building. I was just wondering." Not that her answer helped.

Even though there were many builders around, J.J. Builders was the biggest and who most people in Honey Springs used. Plus, they were Cane Contractors' biggest client.

"We've got to get going." The word *go* sent Pepper into a doggie tizzy. He yelped and jumped around. "I'll see you at the meeting."

We said our goodbyes. I put Pepper in the basket along with the to-go bag of goodies to take to Patrick before I went to the Southern Women's meeting. I was going to use Aunt Maxi's famous saying: "The way to a man's heart is cooking." I'd never served Patrick anything he didn't like.

CHAPTER FOURTEEN

"*I*'m telling you that something isn't right at the bank." I stood on the back deck of Patrick's house, overlooking Lake Honey Springs and watching Timmy play with his trucks. Sassy laid right next to him.

"You know Debbie is going to kill you for giving him those cookies before supper. This is my supper, now." Patrick ignored me.

"Look at tonight two ways." I held two fingers up to him and leaned on the deck railing. "You are helping the love birds have a great date night and go public with their relationship." I was talking about Bib and Babette. "And you are helping me find out some information on the murder of Hillary Canter."

"I can't believe Spencer had the nerve to ask you to look into it." A shadow of annoyance crossed his face.

"He didn't ask me to look into anything." I wanted to clarify. "He asked me to keep my ear to the ground for gossip, and there's got to be plenty of gossip about Hillary at this meeting, especially since her mother is a member."

"You really think her mother is going to be at the meeting?" he asked.

"Well, no, but rumors will be flying." At least I hoped they would be. "I'd like to hear what they have to say."

"Of course, you do," he replied with heavy sarcasm.

"What does that mean?" I asked with a vague sense of disapproval in how he was treating me.

"It means that I wished you'd spend more time planning a date for our wedding than looking into the death of a bridesmaid in Pam's wedding," he muttered.

"So this is the truth behind your coldness to me?" The truth came out. When I noticed Timmy was looking up at us, I knew it was a mistake to fight in front of him. "We aren't going to talk about this right now."

"You never want to talk about it." His voice grew louder when I walked inside. "You stay right here, buddy."

Moments later, he was inside with me.

"You always run when I want to discuss the wedding." He wasn't going to let it go. "You either want to get married, or you don't. What are we waiting on?"

"I've got to go." I pulled on the light jacket that I'd taken off when I got to his house. "We can discuss this later."

"Whatever." He jerked the door open.

"Wait a second." I put my hand on the door that he was closing behind me when I stepped out of the house. "Are you taking out your anger on me because of this thing Cane Contractors has with one of its clients?"

"How did you know about that?" he asked.

"Keeping my ear to the ground." I drove into the ground why Spencer thought I was valuable.

"Your mother." He stared at me. "She called about me putting a lien on a house of her client's because I've not been paid for the work I've done for her house."

"Is this something I should be worried about?" I asked.

"If you're asking this is tied to the bank, no." He shook his head. "This one house isn't going to hurt us. That is if there's a future us."

"Patrick." I took a step closer to him and reached out to grab his hand. "There's nothing wrong with us. I moved to Honey Springs to a new house, opened a new coffeehouse, and reconnected to you while I was still nursing the wounds of my divorce." I stared into his beautiful brown eyes, feeling warm inside. "This past year, I've loved getting my roots planted here, being engaged to you, and owning a thriving business. It's been a lot of change. Great changes. I do want to get married to you. I was just letting those roots grow to make sure everything is grounded." I curled up on my toes and kissed his soft lips. "Let's have supper at the cabin tomorrow night, and we can come up with a date."

"You promise you won't cancel because the bowling team has a rumor about this murder?" he asked.

"Is there really a bowling team?" I asked with my interest piqued.

"No, Roxy. I was joking." He pulled me closer in his arms. It was the safest place I'd been all day.

CHAPTER FIFTEEN

*I*n the great state of Kentucky, the weather was hot one minute, cold the next or raining in the morning with snow in the evening. It was very unpredictable between seasons. Tonight was no different.

On my way back into town to go to the library, rain started to spit from the sky. It wasn't one that made me put the wipers on full blast, but was annoying enough to dot the windshield in the middle of my line of vision.

The sunset against the wet grass turned the countryside a dusty, southern green. "April showers bring May flowers" wasn't only true, it was spot on. Even the bluegrass we are known for became even more vibrant as the rain fed the limestone underneath the ground.

The library was part of the community college, and I wasn't able to see any cars that I recognized because the college kids' cars and all the others were mixed together. I did try to rubberneck to find Morgan's car, but with the rain and the darkening sky, it was a lost cause. I gave up and headed inside.

White marquee letters on a stand spelled out: *Southern Woman's Club meeting this way*, along with a paper arrow pointing in the direction of the one and only conference room in the library.

The smell of bound books and pages was as strong a sensory reminder of how much I loved books as much as the smell of freshly brewed coffee reminded me of how much I loved coffee. Those were two distinct smells that made me feel warm and fuzzy.

"What on earth are you doing here?" Loretta's Southern voice asked.

"I'm the guest of Morgan Keys tonight. I thought I might try out the club and see if it's for me." I shrugged and looked around. I didn't see Morgan.

"If it's not good enough for Maxine, it certainly won't be good enough for you." Loretta put her hand up to her gold chain necklace, which had a turquoise pendant that was the size of a baseball hanging off of it.

"That necklace goes great with your coloring." Morgan rushed in. "It really pops against your tan."

"Tan?" Loretta rolled her eyes so hard, I swear she hurt herself. "This is not a tan. I'm Cherokee. I thought you knew that."

"Really?" Morgan's head tilted, and she furrowed her brows. "Cherokee?"

"As in Naaa-tive American." She put her hand, which had a matching ring to the necklace, on her hip, and the wrinkles around her lips tightened.

"Yes, thank you. I know what that is." Morgan glared back at Loretta. "So, tell me about this big story you went to Maxine Bloom about for the newspaper."

"I only told her what I knew because people in Honey Springs want to know what's going on." She pointed her finger at me. "Ask Roxy. She was there. She might even know more because I left Pam with her in the bathroom."

Morgan looked at me. I shook my head.

"You also told the sheriff." I wasn't going to let her get away with thinking that her finger-pointing was going to get Pam arrested. "Now, he said that Pam is their number-one suspect."

"Well, she did have that fight with her." Loretta wasn't going down without a fight. "And from what I heard, she and Truman were having some issues because of Hillary."

"I can't believe this!" The gasp was heard clear across town when everyone turned to see who was yelling. "I hate this town!" Pam was at the door of the room, but she bolted out.

"Nice going," I said to Loretta. I followed Pam out to the parking lot, where she was fumbling with the keys to her car.

"Just go away, Roxy." She didn't bother looking at me. She jammed the key into the door lock and turned it. "I just want to be left alone."

"I was married before." I knew if I could get her to slow down, I might be able to talk to her and make her feel better. "We got divorced because he cheated on me. If the rumors are true, at least you know now. It'll save you from heartache later."

When she didn't move, I could tell she was listening.

"I'm sorry. Rumors can be so harmful." I could feel the pain radiating off of her. The rain was still at a spit, but it looked like it was going to turn into a downpour at any minute.

"Hillary hit on Truman. He told me about it the night it happened." Pam gulped back tears. "I even forgave her for it in my heart, but I never mentioned it to her. I figured after the wedding, slowly I'd back away from her. But after what she said in public to me, I knew she wanted my life."

"Why don't we go back to the coffeehouse and have a cup of coffee? Plus, I have some things to bake, and you can help me. It always makes me feel better." I reached out and patted her arm.

"Are you sure?" she asked.

"I wouldn't have asked if I wasn't." I offered a sympathetic smile. "Besides, these Southern women are too uppity for me. I like more of a hillbilly style." I winked and filled with joy after she laughed.

"I'll follow you." She opened her car door.

I called Mama on my way to the coffeehouse because it was the only time I was going to have to talk to her. I had to call Patrick when I got home to make sure we were good, and I had a big day tomorrow. I'd already decided that after I got the shop open and Bunny settled, I was going to drive to Lexington to make a visit to Bank Lending Mortgage.

"You know that I'm the suspect now." Pam had taken a seat on one of the stools at the counter. "I didn't do it."

"I don't think you did." I flipped on one of the coffee pots and made a mental note to refill it before I left for the night, since it was the carafe the afternoon girls had filled before they left.

There was a checklist that I required the employees to check off before they closed so I'd be able to walk in the next morning and get started without having to refill salt shakers on the table and take care of little things like napkins and straws. The coffee pots were all ready to go, so I only had to flip on a switch.

"Do you like jam cake?" I asked, not really knowing what I planned to bake when I got her here.

"Yes. I love it. It's very hard to find, though." She sat up on the edge of the stool and waited patiently with the ceramic coffee mug in front of her.

"What if I teach you my family's secret recipe?" I asked and nodded for her to follow me into the kitchen. My heart jumped when I passed Pepper's empty dog bed, and I wondered how he was doing at home alone. I hated to leave him, but it wasn't appropriate to take him some places. Not all people loved dogs—and those were the people I never trusted.

"I know there's a lot of rumors going around about the murder and people pointing fingers at one another." I wasn't sure how to get to the matter of Hillary, but I knew I wanted to know. It was the break I'd been waiting for. I could give Spencer to look at someone different. "Why don't you start from the beginning, as in, with how long you've known Hillary."

She talked while I gathered the dry ingredients from the shelves.

"We met at the Southern Women's Club, of all places." She laughed. "My mom and her mom were members, and they'd put us in the children's section of the library to play while they had their meetings. It was natural for us to grow up and become good friends."

125

I grabbed a bowl on my way over to the shelf to put the items in and carry them over. It was much easier than trying to pack them in my arms. Flour, sugar, raisins, baking soda, and baking powder was the first things I took off the shelves. "That's got to be some really good memories." I carried the bowl back and emptied it onto the steel work-space table. "If you want to grab the buttermilk and blackberry jam out of the refrigerator, that'd be a big help."

"There were some really good memories." She opened the refrigerator and took out the items. "Until her parents started their side business company, and her father was making more and more money. They started to give her everything she ever wanted."

"They own a company?" I asked.

"Yes. Something with the tourist cabins here. Bank Lending Mortgages." She put the wet ingredients on the table. "Anything else?" she asked.

"Yeah." I gulped back my thoughts when she said "Bank Lending Mortgages." It was the mortgage company Mama's client had used and the teller had given me information about. "I need three eggs, nutmeg, cinnamon, and vanilla from the spice shelf."

While she got the ingredients, she continued to tell me about the evolution of her relationship with Hillary. My thoughts were so loud that I didn't hear her.

"Can you excuse me for a minute?" I asked her. "I need to go to the bathroom."

"Sure. I think I heard the coffee pot beep. Can I get a cup?" she asked on our way back out of the swinging door into the coffeehouse.

"Yes. Help yourself." I hurried over to the bathroom and turned the water on the faucet, dialing Spencer.

"Spencer, where are you?" I whispered. "Listen, I know it's late. I really think something fishy is going down at the bank, and it's tied to Hillary's death. Her dad owns Bank Lending Mortgages. I'm not sure how yet, but I think that either her uncle or her father had been doing some underhanded check fraud. I never had a case for check fraud when I was a lawyer, but I do have one of my mom's clients who has a lien against her house and a double mortgage that she didn't do. It's all tied to the bank and J.J. Builders. Call me, and I'll give you the details." I paused. "Maybe someone killed her to get back at her dad. Just a thought."

I hung up the phone. As sure as I was about how delicious my mama's jam cakes was, I was just as sure that somehow Hillary Canter's murder had to do with her father's business dealings.

CHAPTER SIXTEEN

hile Pam and I enjoyed the warm, out-of-the oven jam cake with more coffee, she told me how she and Hillary had remained friends, but that Hillary began to make her feel like a charity case.

She also said that no matter how much money Hillary was fed by her parents, Hillary craved the old life that had resembled Pam's, down to Pam's engagement to Truman. She was going to meet with Emily and Babette this morning because she'd broken off the wedding to Truman. She hadn't canceled the engagement, but they'd decided to go through counseling, assuming that she wasn't going to be arrested for Hillary's murder.

The more she talked, the more I knew that she didn't do it, and somehow Hillary's killer had to do with her family's dealings, which made my drive to Lexington to visit Bank Lending Mortgages even more important. I had to go on my gut. Since I'd not heard from Spencer, I assumed he was checking in on the details I'd given him over the phone.

"You want to know what I heard at the Southern Women's Club?" Morgan had stopped in before I'd even gotten the morning treats for Camey down at the Cocoon in the oven. She was leaned up against the counter in the kitchen and eating a piece of one of the leftover jam cakes that Pam and I had made the night before.

"Yes, I do." I took a few of the tomato and spinach quiches out of the freezer to pop them in the oven. They were the perfect treats for the guests at the inn to enjoy with a cup of coffee. They were light but filling enough to get them started with their day. The quiches would tide them over until the breakfast Camey provided was ready.

"That looks good." She eyed the pie plates full of quiche when I walked by.

"The story?" I reminded her. I put them in the oven. I set the timer.

"After you ran after Pam, I'd heard that Truman had cheated on her with Hillary. Did she say anything to you about it?" she asked.

"She did, but I think Hillary actually made a pass at him." I grabbed the pot and poured myself a cup of coffee. "If she did it, why would she meet her so early? What would be the point of that?"

"According to Loretta, the Canters are having some financial problems and trying to get Hillary married off as quickly as possible." She took a sip of her coffee.

"Do you know anything about their business?" I asked, pretending that I didn't know anything about the business. I walked over to Pepper's kibble and put a scoop in his bowl.

He quickly ate it up then went to lie in his bed for a nap.

"Not much. I remember when I was little, they started buying up all the lake front property and helped get Lake Honey Springs popular with boaters by building the log cabins. From there, I think they just grew and grew." She shrugged. "Bank Lending Mortgages."

"What about the uncle that works down at the Honey Springs National Bank?" I asked.

"I don't know much about him. You'd think he'd be more involved with more committees since he's the president of the bank, but he's never been involved with anything but growing the bank. Loretta did say that her husband had some sort of big trustee meeting."

"What do the trustees do?" I asked.

"From what Loretta had said, there was some sort of issue with a loan, and they had to vote on it." She gave out some good information. I wondered if Aunt Maxi knew who was on the board—and if she'd talked to them.

"I went to the bank, and I talked to Mr. Rich, Emily's dad. She runs the Bee's Knees Bakery. He told me that they had to call in some of their loans."

What was the tie to Hillary Canter's murder? That was my question. The whole thing was a big puzzle, and I was missing the most crucial piece.

"Really? That's why you asked me who owned my building." She lowered her eyes. We stared at each other for a second. "Are you thinking this has something to do with Hillary's murder?"

"I think there's a tie somewhere. Why on earth would anyone want to meet in the middle of the night?" I asked.

"You also said she had on the coat Babette and she were fighting over. How did she get the coat if Babette didn't give it to her?" Then, she asked a question I was afraid I was never going to be able to answer. "Someone had to have given her the coat."

"Do you know who owns All in The Details's building?" I asked.

"At one time, I know that J.J. Builders owned them, but with the revitalization, we had the option of buying the shop or leasing it. I think she bought it. Cane Contractors might have bought some, too." She drummed her fingers on the counter. "When is that quiche going to be done? I'd like to take a piece to go."

With Morgan and her to-go quiche out of the coffeehouse, I gave Aunt Maxi a quick call. Her voicemail answered, and I was glad to have some space on it to leave a message.

"Aunt Maxi, I really think that there is a tie between Hillary's murder and the building business. A lot of loans are being called in from the bank. They wouldn't do that unless they were in over their heads. I heard they were having a trustee meeting or something. I'm hoping you know someone on the board. Check it out and call me." I hung up the phone.

After Bunny got to work, Pepper and I took the quiche and coffee down to Camey at the Cocoon Inn. On our way back, I wanted to talk to Babette about her building. There were three things in the South that people didn't want to discuss: politics, religion, and money. I hoped Babette would give me a little insight into the finances around her building because I clearly remember her saying that she had to have Pam's wedding.

There was a note taped to the door that said she'd be back in a couple of hours. I couldn't help but wonder how her date night went with Bib and if it was extended all night and until today, especially if the big event she was working on was Pam's wedding.

My phone chirped from my back pocket.

"Good morning," I greeted Patrick, excited that he'd called.

"Good morning." His deep, Southern voice was music to my ears. "I'm sorry about last night. I was just too tired from watching Timmy and when you called so late, I was grumpy."

"I should've texted to let you know that I was with Pam most of the night because she was upset about being suspect in Hillary's murder and that she called the wedding off." I opened the door to the Bean Hive, and Pepper rushed right in ahead of me.

Bunny was chit-chatting with the customers, and they all seemed to be pretty happy.

"That's a bummer. I feel bad for them. I guess the rumor about Truman is not a rumor?" He asked.

"She said it was Hillary who made the pass, not Truman, as Hillary made it sound." I recalled the sadness on Pam's face and remembered that awful feeling.

I checked on the tea and coffee bars to make sure they were well stocked. Then I looked at the array of treats in the glass counter to see if they needed a refill. It appeared Bunny was on top of things.

"The jam cake is a hit." She wiggled her brows when she saw what I was doing.

I gave her the thumbs-up and walked back into the kitchen to get the soup ready for lunch. I wanted to make sure that I could focus on Bank Lending Mortgages when I drove to Lexington, instead of getting a million phone calls from Bunny. There were pots on the stove, filled with the soup. Bunny had already gotten that started, too. She was a lifesaver for me.

I grabbed my keys off the hook and did one final check of the coffeehouse before I waved bye to Bunny. She'd also agreed to take care of Pepper.

"Also, I'm sorry I didn't tell Penny about the lien I put on her client. I've got our lawyers looking into it this morning, and I probably should've checked with Penny about it." Patrick was good at recognizing when he was crabby. It was cute how he tried to apologize.

Last night's rain had made way for a sunny and warm day. It felt refreshing to have the sun beat down on me on my way to the car. Pepper and I had driven in this morning because I knew I wanted to head to Lexington.

"I think there's more to it than you." There was a knot in my stomach. "I went to see Evan Rich at the bank to apologize for talking him into letting Emily start the bakery. I'd thought she was closing the bakery because she wasn't mature financially, but in reality, the bank has called her loan, and she can't pay it in full. Then there's Mama's client, who has a second mortgage on her house that she didn't take out."

"Are you telling me that the bank is doing some sort of laundering?" There was valid concern in Patrick's voice. "Because all my money is tied up there, and there's a huge problem if that's the case."

"I'm not sure, but Mama hired me to look into it as a lawyer." I wasn't sure if I should tell him I was going to Lexington to see if I could get some answers from the mortgage company, but I knew that if I was going to be honest and open in our relationship and move past the engagement to an actual date, I had to tell him. "That's why I'm getting in my car right now to drive to Lexington."

"You have an appointment there?" He asked.

"I'm going to Bank Lending Mortgages to see what I can find out. When I was at Honey Springs National Bank, I gave the teller Mama's client's information, and she said that she'd heard the mortgage company fired the girl who did some closings because they were investigating her depositing the closing checks into a personal account."

"Whose personal account?" he asked with an eager voice.

"I don't know that yet, but I'm planning on finding out. Maybe it wasn't a personal account so much as J.J. Builders." There was a little more traffic than usual, so I took a few of the back roads to drive around the town and miss most of the tourist traffic. "I also want to find out who the girl they fired is. I want to talk to her."

"I put in a call to Shepard because, like you, I feel like something might be going on, and if I'm the only person they've done it to, then I can stop them." He was right. The only incident I knew of was this one with him and Mama's client.

"I'll see what answers I get, and I'll call you back on my way home. I'm sure you're right." I wanted to make us both feel better, but I'd seen before that when there was one money laundering crime, there were usually more. "I bet this just an isolated case, and maybe the girl who worked for the mortgage company accidentally deposited it."

Lexington was the biggest city near Honey Springs. It was the city that had all the good clothing shops and more than just mom-and-pop restaurants like we had in Honey Springs. It was a special treat for Patrick and me to make a real date night when we planned to visit the city.

The Bank Lending Mortgages office was in the tall, blue-glass building on Main Street. There was a parking garage attached to it, and I wasn't about to drive around the block several times just to look for an empty spot. I paid the ten-dollar parking-lot fee and found a spot pretty close to the elevators.

I looked down at my phone and saw that the time was already noon. I wondered why I'd not heard from Spencer yet and realized the bars on my phone showed there was no service. You'd think with all the new technology, someone would have come up with something to provide service in parking garages by now.

I grabbed the file Mama gave me and threw my phone in my messenger bag.

"Ouch." I pulled my hand out when something sharp poked me. I looked into my bag and realized the pin on Timmy's sheriff badge had poked my finger. I rubbed the tip of my finger and strapped the messenger bag across my chest.

There was a chest-high desk with a man sitting behind it that in the entryway of the building.

"Can I help you?" he asked when I got off the elevator.

"I've got an appointment with Bank Lending Mortgages." I looked past him at the marquee that listed all the businesses in the building.

"Fourth floor." He smiled and gestured to another set of elevators just beyond his desk. "I've not seen many of the workers, but I'm sure someone's up there."

"Thanks for your help," I said. I walked down the hall to where he'd pointed.

He was right. It was a ghost town up there. There were three rows of grey cubicle walls, and each desk was empty. The sunlight was pouring in from the glass walls and made the inside of the offices toasty.

"Can I help you?" I heard a woman's voice call out to me. She was in the far-left corner of the room.

"I'm looking for Bank Lending Mortgages. I don't think I'm in the right office." I turned to walk out.

"You're in the right spot. They're gone." She got my attention. "I'm just here to clean up the space so it can be leased again."

"Do you know what happened? Did they move?" I asked, walking towards her.

"I just work for the cleaning service." She shrugged. "I'm cleaning out the offices. It looks like they just up and left."

I couldn't help but notice a doorplate on that said "president," and there were boxes with stuff sticking out of them. I opened my messenger bag.

"I'm with the Honey Springs sheriff's department." I jerked Timmy's fake badge of my bag and flashed it quickly before putting it back. "I'm here to go through some of the documents."

"Have at it. I'm just going to throw it all in the dumpster." She moseyed past me with a pushcart and didn't question anything. The wheels on the cart made an eerie squeaking sound each time they rolled one full revolution.

I waited until she'd made it halfway across the offices before I started to look through the first box. There were some pens and pencils with a few awards, but nothing that appeared to be paperwork.

My phone chirped with a text, and I pulled it out. It was from Spencer. He said that he had not been able to call me back, but felt like it was a good idea if I didn't continue to look for information on Hillary's case because I wasn't a trained professional.

I just rolled my eyes and put the phone back in my bag. While the cleaning lady threw items into her pushcart, I continued to look through the next few boxes. Just when I didn't think I had anything, there was something that caught my eye.

"Well, well, well." I took out a framed photo and stared at the young ladies in between the two men. "That's Hillary Canter, her uncle, and"—I didn't recognize the other man, but I did recognize the other girl—"a much younger Jana." I immediately recognized the sales clerk from Queen for a Day.

My heart started to beat rapidly because it was proof that Jana did know Hillary. What did Jana have to do with this man and Hillary's family? Plus, Jana had a connection to the white coat Hillary had on when she was strangled. But what was the connection?

There was only one way to find out.

"It's time I pick up my dress from you." I ran my finger over Jana's face before I slipped the frame into my messenger bag.

CHAPTER SEVENTEEN

he car ride back to Honey Springs was torture. I had to get to Queen for the Day to talk to Jana. I'd called Spencer and left him a message about what I'd found and suggested that maybe he needed to question her. I also called Patrick, who didn't answer, and left him a message about how Bank Lending Mortgages had upped and closed shop. Neither of them had called me back by the time I made it to the parking lot of the boardwalk.

Instead of my leisurely walk along the boardwalk to look out at all the boaters, I shoved my way through the tourists until I got to Queen for the Day.

Jana was behind the counter when I made it into the shop.

"I was wondering if you still wanted that dress, since I'd gotten the email saying that Pam had called the wedding off." Jana smiled so sweetly that I couldn't help but think that maybe the devil was under there.

"She sent out an email?" I asked.

"She sent one to me, Babette, and Emily, I guess since we were each doing something for the wedding. She also said that they aren't broken up, but in light of things, she said they were postponing the wedding and getting some much-needed counseling to make sure they are meant for each other."

I was glad to see that Pam had taken some of my advice. I wanted to check in with her later.

"I guess you don't want the dress? Is that why you're here?" She asked. Then, she let out a belch. "Gosh, excuse me." She blushed and took a drink from the water bottle. "Sometimes"—she hiccupped and giggled—"I get the hiccups."

Hiccups? The memory of hearing a hiccup on Aunt Maxi's voicemail ruffled through my mind like wind on water. When I realized that Morgan had mentioned it, too, my head jerked up, and I looked at Jana as she hiccupped again.

Jana was Hillary's killer. My intuition nipped at my gut.

"Actually"—I opened my messenger bag and pulled out the picture frame—"I didn't realize the night I was here that you and Hillary were friends." I held the picture toward her. "Though she did ask you what you were going to do about it, as if she expected that you would work in her favor. Why was that? Did you owe her something? Was she holding something over your head, so you decided to kill her?"

Her face grew still, and she clenched her teeth. "You have a very active imagination." She let out a nervous laugh. "That's what I told the sheriff, and he seemed not to think I had anything to do with Hillary's death. I didn't know her well. We'd met at a work function and had a photo taken together. I don't think she even remembered it."

"Who is this guy in the photo with you?" I asked, pointing to the man I didn't know. "I know Mr. Canter, Hillary's uncle from the bank, but who is this?"

"That's my dad," she said matter-of-factly. "He's a good man. An honest man. He built up this town when it was in financial ruins." Apparently, Jana had decided to dispense with the pleasantries and met fire with fire. "In fact, this very spot you're standing in and all the shops on this boardwalk wouldn't be here unless my father and his company stepped in and saved it a year ago."

"Hillary's father has gone out of business. I was just there. Someone has been putting the checks into your father's bank account. The money that was supposed to go into the Bank Lending Mortgages account to pay off people's building loans to your father is gone, and now he's in trouble. Hillary knew it, didn't she? That's why you strangled her?"

The last puzzle piece I'd been looking for had just fallen from my mouth, and it was all clear in my head, only I wasn't for sure if she actually strangled Hillary, or if her father did it.

"Did you say you were a lawyer?" She asked, walking backwards and moving toward the door.

"I am. And I think you're going to need one." I continued to bait her, but apparently it wasn't a good move. When she flipped the shop sign on the door to "closed" and locked not only the door lock, but the dead bolt, I figured I might be in a smidgen of trouble. "Let me get my phone and give you some good referrals."

"Your phone?" She walked over and smacked it out of my hands. As if that wasn't enough, she stomped her heel into it. "You think I'm falling for that? You were going to call Spencer."

"I'm right?" I took a step backwards because she walked closer towards me. "You either killed Hillary or know something or someone who did. Maybe your father?"

I had to stop backing up when my heel hit the water compartment of the steamer. I looked down and saw a pink phone floating in the water chamber.

"Is that Hillary's phone?" I asked, trying to steady my quivering voice.

"My father did nothing. She was nosy, and she needed to be stopped." Jana's action told me that there was now a clear declaration of war between us, and I had to win.

"Why did you do it? Why did you kill her?" I had to buy some time so I could figure out how to get past her and out that door.

"When she'd come in here and I didn't have what she wanted, she would say that she knew what I did, and she was going to go to the police if I didn't get her what she wanted." Jana reached for the cord of the steamer and let it dangle from her fingertips.

I gulped, wondering if she wanted to put it around my neck.

"The night she was in here with Babette and wanted the coat, she knew that my family had the extra set of keys to All About the Details. When she saw the coat hanging in the window, she demanded that I get the keys and get her the coat, or she was going to go straight to the police about how I was the one who deposited the checks into my father's account." Her eyes watered. She swallowed and drew her shoulders back. "She made the plan for it to be in the middle of the night so no one would see us."

"What do you mean you deposited the checks?" I asked

She pulled the cord taut with her hands, making a snapping sound.

I jumped.

"I was the loan closer for J.J. Builders, my father's company." All her words began to put the clues about my mama's client together. "At first, I was naive when he told me to just drop off the closing check to Mr. Canter at Honey Springs Bank. It made sense because Mr. Canter's brother, Hillary's father, was the owner of Bank Lending Mortgages. I figured they had it all worked out. Then, I started to get interest-payment statements from Bank Lending Mortgages on these properties I closed. When I asked my father about it, he told me that I just needed to pay the interest because the checks hadn't cleared from the closing."

"Bank Lending Mortgages had no idea the houses had sold because you were sending the interest-only payments on the loan." I had to admit, it was a brilliant cover-up scheme for money laundering.

"I continued to ask my father about it. I quit after I felt terrible about it because I knew these people had second mortgages on their houses, and they didn't know it. Then, the contractors starting coming by to get their money because my father hadn't paid them. They even threatened my father." She snarled and hiccupped.

"Mr. Canter at the bank knew, too?" This scheme was far-reaching and beyond more than just Hillary's demise.

"Oh yeah. My father's bank account overdrew about three million dollars, and they ended up giving him another loan without telling the trustees. They knew my father was going to pay it back, only it caught up to him and all the companies involved." She blazed tightly, with her hands still wrapped around the cord of the steamer. "Hillary came to me about it and told me her father was going to the FBI. I told her I knew nothing, but she knew I did. Then, she said she was going to expose me and send me to jail for my hand in it. The night of the coat, the FBI came by our house. My father had the nerve to ask me to take the fall. Hillary was texting me and telling me that she was going to contact the newspaper if I didn't get that coat for her."

"How did you get the coat?" I asked, trying to think of a way to shove her out of my way to get out.

"Haven't you been listening?" she spat. She hiccupped. "My father's company rebuilt All About the Details, and we still have a set of keys to the back door. We put in the security cameras. I know exactly how they are positioned. I slipped in the back door, out of the views of the cameras, and got the coat."

"You met her in the middle of the night because you didn't want anyone to see you give it to her?" It didn't make sense.

"You're not a very good lawyer. No wonder you brew coffee." Her anger was bubbling, and I could tell she was coming to a head. "I was going to just give her the coat until I realized she was going to continue blackmailing me even after my father was arrested. It had to end with her."

This Southern showdown was about to be over. She took one more step closer to me with that cord, but I knew that if I could get one of her arms, I'd be able to take her down.

"I'm sorry. I kinda liked your coffee." She took another step, but I did, too.

I lifted my arms in the air and focused on grabbing her left forearm and bringing it squarely down on my knee. The cracking sound and her screaming out in pain intense enough to send her to her knees told me that I'd broken her arm. She rolled over on her back, cradling the limp limb.

"I think you broke my arm!" she yelled while she hiccupped.

"You know what?" My shoe slammed into her chest and cut off her breath. "You were right. For a lawyer, I wasn't good. I was great!" I put a little more weight on her chest to make sure she felt my wrath. "That damn hiccup problem you've got is what gave it away. You hiccupped when you killed her, and a couple of people reported that they heard someone hiccup."

The sound of shattering glass made me jump around. The ten hair-raising, heart-pounding minutes of terror were over when I saw Sheriff Shepard Spencer kick in the rest of the glass on the front door and run in with his gun drawn.

The hours that followed were pretty much a blur.

CHAPTER EIGHTEEN

"Then you said what?" Crissy asked.

This time, instead of Bunny Bowowski holding court with all the gossiping citizens who had come into the Bean Hive, folks were there to hear my story about how I took down Hillary Canter's killer.

"I told her I was a damn great lawyer." I dragged the steaming cup of coffee up to my lips and took a sip. I looked over at Pam Horton, Truman Philips, Emily Rich, Big Bib, and Babette Cliff.

Bentley and Pepper had curled up in Pepper's bed. It was good to see that Pepper had finally accepted the Pet Palace adoptee, though it could have been that Bentley seemed a lot calmer.

"And that's not all." Mama nodded. "They arrested Hillary Canter's uncle and Jana's father. All the assets from J.J. Builders are going to pay off the second mortgages, along with the contractors that need to be paid, including Patrick Cane and the Bee's Knees Bakery."

"Thank you, Mama." I gave her a big hug.

"Don't thank me." She pointed at the door when the bell overhead dinged. "Thank your Aunt Maxi. She's the one who blew up the internet and phones with her sleuthing, not to mention endlessly going down to the sheriff's department and bugging them about it."

"Aw, it was nothin'." Aunt Maxi winked. She had on a fedora with a big purple feather sticking out of it, along with a light-purple caftan and a pair of purple ballet slippers. "It was the money that wasn't accounted for that had me thrown for a loop."

"What money was that?" I asked because I knew the checks left a paper trail right into J.J. Builder's account.

"Jana's father had gotten a little too big for his britches." Aunt Maxi pulled out her little newspaper notebook. "He was depositing the loan checks into his account, with the help of Jana, and that's when he started to get greedy. There were big trips and lavish gifts. He figured since all the citizens were using his company, he'd be able to pay back what he took without people knowing. He even cashed a couple checks that totaled up to three hundred thousand dollars. And he buried it forty-one paces off the fifth tee of the Honey Springs Country Club golf course."

"So that's where Spencer had been spending all his time." My jaw dropped. "They were looking for the cash."

Bunny Bowowski meandered around the coffeehouse, refilling the cups with fresh coffee and offering up sweet treats to go with it.

"Jana's father was coming clean, but Jana's decision to kill Hillary was a completely separate crime. Her father only confessed to stealing the money because he thought if he could pay back some of the three million he'd embezzled, he'd get a shorter sentence." Aunt Maxi was good at this stuff. Much better than I figured her for. "Spencer had no idea the two crimes were paired until I got that call from Hillary the night she was murdered. He said that he went to see Jana at Queen for the Day to ask about her father, and she started to get the hiccups."

"Oh, yeah. Dead giveaway," I said.

"He couldn't obviously match the hiccups in my voicemail from Hillary to Jana's, but decided to see if she'd gone to the doctor. He subpoenaed her records." Aunt Maxi's voice went down an octave and she got real mysterious. "The doctor said that when Jana gets nervous, she gets a case of the hiccups—since she was a little girl."

"He put two and two together." I smiled, thankful I took Jana down before she strangled me.

"Poor Hillary. She never saw it coming. According to the coroner's report." Aunt Maxi dug down into her messenger bag then took out the file. "Hillary was strangled from behind."

The room was met with gasps.

"Now that it's over, we can enjoy the summer tourists and get back to normal," I proclaimed, holding my cup up in the air. "To Aunt Maxi."

There was a round of "here, here."

"I've got an announcement," Babette said as she stood. "I've decided that Bentley belongs with me. He rounds out the three B's." She pointed to herself, then Bib, then Bentley. "Babette, Bib, and Bentley."

"That's wonderful news!" I rushed over and hugged her. "I knew he was a perfect fit. That's why I asked you to take him for a while."

"I have even more news." Pam stood up and rested her hand on Truman's shoulder. "Truman and I are going through with the wedding. It's going to be exactly how I've always wanted my wedding to be, and Emily Rich is going to make that beautiful white cake with the pink-and-white flowers I've always wanted."

The news was greeted with everyone giving them well wishes and congratulations. It was my time to slip out of the limelight and let Pam have the attention she so well deserved.

"Good job, baby." Warm and familiar arms slipped around my waist from behind.

"When did you get here?" I turned around and smiled at Patrick.

"I came in the back door, and I didn't want to disturb the fun y'all seemed to be having." He winked. "I'm proud of you."

"You are?" I asked.

"I am." He gave me a kiss. "I'm not getting all my money back, but I'll get at least some."

"Where's Timmy?" I asked when I didn't see him with Patrick since I knew he was watching him for Debbie.

"Debbie found a new babysitter." He pulled at my engagement ring finger and looked at the beautiful ring he'd given me. "What about that date?"

"I've always loved the fall weather in Kentucky. And the trees are gorgeous around the Cocoon Inn that time of the year for an outdoor wedding." I'd given him a date.

He picked me up and swung me around.

"Roxanne Bloom, you've just made me the happiest man alive." He squeezed me tighter, setting my decision in stone.

"Did I hear you right?" Aunt Maxi didn't miss a beat. I smiled at her. "Now, when am I gonna get a grandniece?"

"Don't start that," I warned. But I knew that since we'd set a date, she was going to bug me about a baby.

THE END

If you enjoyed reading this book as much as I enjoyed writing it then be sure to return to the Amazon page and leave a review.

Go to Tonyakappes.com for a full reading order of my novels and while there join my newsletter. You can also find links to Facebook, Instagram and Goodreads.

Keep reading for a sneak peek of the next book in the series. Decaffeinated Scandal is now available to purchase on Amazon.

From Tonya: Oh...real quick before you keep scrolling. I've got a story for y'all. A real story.

Whooo hooo!! I'm so glad we are a week out from last Coffee Chat with Tonya and happy to report the poison ivy is almost gone! But y'all we got more issues than Time magazine up in our family.

When y'all ask me if my real life ever creeps into books, well...grab your coffee because here is a prime example!

My sweet mom's birthday was over the weekend. Now, I'd already decided me and Rowena was going to stay there for a couple of extra days.

On her birthday, Sunday, Tracy and David were there too, and we were talking about what else...poison ivy! I was telling them how I can't stand not shaving my legs. Mom and Tracy told me they don't shave daily and I might've curled my nose a smidgen. And apparently it didn't go unnoticed.

I went inside the house to start cooking breakfast for everyone and mom went up to her room to get her bathing suit on and Tracy was with me. All the men were already outside on the porch.

The awfulest crash came from upstairs and my sister tore out of that kitchen like a bat out of hell and I kept flipping the bacon. My mom had fallen...shaving her legs!

Great. Now it's my fault.

Her wrist was a little stiff but she kept saying she was fine. We had a great day. We celebrated her birthday, swam, and had cake. When it came time for everyone to leave but me and Ro, I told mom that she should probably go get an x-ray because her wrist was a little swollen.

After a lot of coaxing, she agreed and I put my shoes on and told Tracy, David, and Eddy to go on home and we'd call them.

My mama looked me square in the face and said, "You're going with that top knot on your head?"

I said, "yes."

She sat back down in the chair and said, "I'm not going with you lookin' like that."

"Are you serious?" I asked.

"Yes. I'm dead serious. I'm not going with you looking like that. What if we see someone?" She was serious, y'all!

She protested against my hair!

Now...this is exactly like the southern mama's I write about! I looked at Eddy and he was laughing. Tracy and David were laughing and I said, "I can't wait until I tell my coffee chat people about this."

As you can see in the above photo, the before and after photo.

Yep...we went and she broke her wrist! Can you believe that? We were a tad bit shocked, and I'll probably be staying a few extra days (which will give us even more to talk about over coffee next week).

Oh...we didn't see anyone we knew so I could've worn my top knot! As I'm writing this, you can bet your bottom dollar my hair is pulled up in my top knot!

Okay, so y'all might be asking why I'm putting this little story in the back of my book, well, that's a darn tootin' good question.

This is exactly what you can expect when you sign up for my newsletter. There's always something going on in my life that I have to chat with y'all about each Tuesday on Coffee Chat with Tonya. Go to Tonyakappes.com and click on subscribe in the upper right corner to join.

Chapter One of Book Five
Decaffeinated Scandal

"It's looking like you're going to be ready after all." I stood on the steps of The Cocoon Inn with one hand gripping a commercial coffee carafe and the other holding a to-go Bean Hive coffeehouse box filled with Lunch Lady Brownie Bars.

"I'm not sure, but Camey sure is working me like crazy." "I'm not sure there are enough hours in the day, but I'm doin' my best." Newton Oakley hunched over the flowerbed next to the front steps, digging up enough dirt to place an orange mum. Pepper, my curious little Schnauzer, was standing next to him, watching his every move.

Newton sat back on his haunches, took his gloves off, and gave Pepper a few scratches under his salt and pepper beard.

"I think we're all working hard to make sure this year's Neewollah Festival is the best yet." The name of our three day fall festival – Halloween backwards – still did not roll off my tongue easily. It was something I was going to have to learn to say since making the small, quaint town of Honey Springs, Kentucky, my home. "You be sure you grab a cup of coffee this morning. It's a new fall blend that I'm sure you're going to love."

"I'll have to come in and warm up after I get this row of mums planted." He gestured over his shoulders at the orange, yellow, and red mums sitting in the leafy grass behind him, ready to be planted.

"Good morning!" Camey Montgomery met me at the top of the steps. There was a plaid blanket draped over her forearm. "Let me throw this on the rocking chair and I'll help you."

The sound of Camey's voice made Pepper dart up the steps. My nosey little dog loved everyone, but he particularly loved Camey. She was the treat lady.

"I've got it." I protested, but she'd already put the blanket over one of the many white rocking chairs lining the large plantation porch.

"Don't be silly." She pushed her long red hair over one shoulder and took the box from me. "I can't risk you dropping my box of goodies," she laughed and nodded towards the door.

"Every time I walk in here, it still takes my breath away." Pepper and I stepped into the white mansion, built circa 1841, that was situated right on Lake Honey Springs and I turned around to look out one of the floor to ceiling windows that offered guests a spectacular view.

"Yeah. I'm so lucky," she said, reaching into the bowl of dog treats she kept on the counter for the furry guests that accompanied their families.

"Yes, you are." I heard the familiar voice of Walker Peavler, Honey Springs' most recent transplant.

"Walker." I couldn't stop smiling while he and Camey embraced into a sweet kiss on the lips. "I've not seen you in a while, but I've seen Amelia. I can't believe how she's grown."

Walker had been a single man with custody of his granddaughter. He'd stolen Camey's heart while staying at the Cocoon Inn. Since he had a sales job and traveled all the time, he could live anywhere. It truly was a perfect union. He and Camey were both in their fifties and Honey Springs was a fantastic place to raise a child. If you didn't know their back story and saw Walker, Camey, and Amelia out and about around town, you'd never know that Amelia wasn't Camey's biological granddaughter. The only thing the three of them did not share was the same last name. Camey had decided to keep her last name when they got married due to her business and how much time it'd take to get all the documents changed.

"Amelia sure is something special." He leaned back and looked into the hospitality room. "She's going to be late for school if she doesn't hurry up."

"She's eating her oatmeal. Run upstairs and grab her coat." Camey shooed him off to their living quarters in the inn.

I followed her into the hospitality room where I replaced the commercial coffee carafe with the new one. The focal point of the room was a large, beautiful fireplace directly across from the entryway. A few snaps and pops filled the room as the wood crackled in the fireplace, making the unseasonably cool morning cozy and the room very inviting.

"Roxy! Pepper!" Amelia jumped up from a small café table and ran over to greet us. "Did you see my pumpkin?" She giggled as Pepper gave her a sweet kiss along her nose.

"I didn't, but I know without seeing it that it's going to win the pumpkin carving contest." I bent down and gave her a hug. Pepper demanded one too, so of course I gave him one.

"Your granddaddy went to grab your coat, so you better eat up before you're late to school." Camey gave Amelia a scrub on the head with her fingertips, sending her back to the table. "She's more excited about the pumpkins than her costume."

"To be a kid again." I laughed and took the box of brownie bars from Camey. "I'll get these arranged and then I've got to get back. I left Bunny alone."

"Oh, dear." Camey and I both knew my senior citizen assistant, Bunny Bowowski, wasn't the best person to leave alone. "I hope the Bean Hive is still standing when you get back."

Both of us laughed, me a little more nervously than her.

"Let's go, squirt." Walker shook the lightweight coat with an extended arm, summoning Amelia.

"Don't forget to look at my pumpkin," she reminded me as she darted past us. "Love you, mama," she called to Camey. "Bye, Pepper."

"I love you too. Have a great day," Camey called out to Amelia.

"Come down to the coffeehouse later and I'll let you take Pepper for a walk." I waved goodbye.

"I will," Amelia said with a giggle and waved over her granddad as he lifted her in the air and placed her over his shoulder.

"I'm so happy for you," I said to Camey as I arranged the brownies on the three-tiered platter. "You look so happy and content."

"I am and I can't wait for you to join us." She peeked around my arm and reached for a brownie. "Have you and Patrick set a date yet?"

"We have plans to meet that Justice of the Peace, Brandy Cliff." The thought of marrying Patrick Cane sent a wave of joy through my body that I never thought I would experience.

I had been married once before and it wasn't pretty. I knew when he asked me to marry him something was off when I didn't get the giggles and squeals. But with Patrick, I instantly knew the first time I saw him and that was when we were teens. Life went on and we ended up losing touch. Here we were eleven years later and happy as could be.

"I told him it was fine for Brandy to perform the ceremony, like she did for you and Walker. I've gone through one marriage and another lifetime to get back to Honey Springs, so any way I become Roxanne Bloom Cane is perfect for me." I smacked Camey's hand away when she went for another brownie. "If you don't stop, your customers aren't going to get any."

"It's crazy. I've been craving chocolate and I just can't get enough of your fresh baked goodies." She licked her lips and brushed her hands together. "I better get to work before I lose my customers."

"You're not going to lose anyone. Not only do they love you, but you're the only place for them to stay during the Neewollah Festival." I picked up the empty coffee carafe and followed her out to the entrance.

"Not from what I hear." She shook her head with a frown on her face.

"What did you hear?" Apparently, the gossip hadn't gotten to me yet, which was unusual.

"There's been this guy snooping around the courthouse and PVA office about land near or on Honey Springs Lake. Asking about how the economy is each season." She gnawed on the edge of her lip as she referred to the Property Valuation Administration office.

"A guy?" I questioned. "There are a lot of tourists that come into the Bean Hive asking about our small town, but it was just chit-chat. I'd chalk it up to just being nosey."

Her brows pulled. "Some property along the lake over at the Bee Farm."

"The Bee Farm?" The more she talked, the more confused I got.

"Ask around today," she leaned over and whispered as a mom and dad and their little boy walked up to the check in desk.

It wasn't the whispering that made me want to call my mom right away, but the quick head nod Camey had gestured towards the family standing inside her inn. My mom was a local realtor, so maybe she'd heard.

"Have a good day, Roxy," Newton called as I hurried down the steps to get back to the coffeehouse. He'd only gotten a couple more mums planted.

"Bye!" I yelled, with a ton of questions in my mind about the possibility of the Bee Farm selling its land. "Come on, Pepper."

Decaffeinated Scandal is now available to purchase on Amazon.

RECIPES FROM THE BEAN HIVE

Mama's Jam Cake
Best Friends Frappe Coffee

Mama's Jam Cake

(This is straight out of Tonya's mama's own private cookbook. Tonya and her sister fight over the family cookbook that's still in her mama's grips.)

Ingredients

- 1 ¾ cups all purpose flour
- 1 ½ cups white sugar
- 1 cup canola oil
- 1 cup buttermilk
- 1 cup raisins
- 1 cup blackberry jam
- 1 tsp. baking soda
- 1 tsp. baking powder
- 1 tsp cinnamon
- 1 tsp nutmeg
- 1 tsp cloves/allspice
- ½ tsp salt
- 1 tsp vanilla
- 1 cup pecans
- 3 eggs

Directions

1. Preheat oven to 350 degrees
2. Spray two-9 inch cake pans.
3. In a bowl, combine all ingredients except the pecans.
4. Mix well on high speed with a hand mixer. Add pecans to the mixer.
5. Fill both pans with cake mix evenly.
6. Bake 40 minutes or until done. Ovens vary.

Carmel Icing Ingredients

- 2 ¼ cups brown sugar
- 1 ½ tsp butter
- 2 tsp vanilla
- 3 tsp white corn syrup
- 4 ½ tsp milk
- 2 ¼ cups confectioners sugar

Directions

1. Melt everything except the confectioners sugar together on low in a small pot. Stir until all mixed.
2. Add confectioners sugar and cool.
3. Once cooled, spread on the cakes.
4. You can add a few whole pecans to the top for decoration or not. Bakers choice.

Best Friends Frappe Coffee

Ingredients

- 1/4 cup instant coffee granules
- 1/2 cup chocolate syrup
- 1/4 cup sugar
- 1 1/2 cups boiling water
- 2 cups half-and-half
- 1 quart vanilla ice cream
- 2 cups ginger ale Vanilla ice cream, optional

Directions

1. Stir together first 4 ingredients in a large pitcher; cool.
2. Cover and chill at least 8 hours.
3. Stir together coffee mixture, half-and-half, and 1 quart ice cream in a punch bowl.
4. Stir in ginger ale, pour into glasses.
5. Top with ice cream, if desired.

BOOKS BY TONYA
SOUTHERN HOSPITALITY WITH A SMIDGEN OF HOMICIDE

Camper & Criminals Cozy Mystery Series

All is good in the camper-hood until a dead body shows up in the woods.

BEACHES, BUNGALOWS, AND BURGLARIES
DESERTS, DRIVING, & DERELICTS
FORESTS, FISHING, & FORGERY
CHRISTMAS, CRIMINALS, AND CAMPERS
MOTORHOMES, MAPS, & MURDER
CANYONS, CARAVANS, & CADAVERS
HITCHES, HIDEOUTS, & HOMICIDES
ASSAILANTS, ASPHALT & ALIBIS
VALLEYS, VEHICLES & VICTIMS
SUNSETS, SABBATICAL AND SCANDAL
TENTS, TRAILS AND TURMOIL
KICKBACKS, KAYAKS, AND KIDNAPPING
GEAR, GRILLS & GUNS
EGGNOG, EXTORTION, AND EVERGREEN
ROPES, RIDDLES, & ROBBERIES
PADDLERS, PROMISES & POISON
INSECTS, IVY, & INVESTIGATIONS
OUTDOORS, OARS, & OATH
WILDLIFE, WARRANTS, & WEAPONS
BLOSSOMS, BBQ, & BLACKMAIL
LANTERNS, LAKES, & LARCENY
JACKETS, JACK-O-LANTERN, & JUSTICE
SANTA, SUNRISES, & SUSPICIONS
VISTAS, VICES, & VALENTINES
ADVENTURE, ABDUCTION, & ARREST

Holiday Cozy Mystery Series

CELEBRATE GOOD CRIMES!

FOUR LEAF FELONY
MOTHER'S DAY MURDER
A HALLOWEEN HOMICIDE
NEW YEAR NUISANCE
CHOCOLATE BUNNY BETRAYAL
FOURTH OF JULY FORGERY
SANTA CLAUSE SURPRISE
APRIL FOOL'S ALIBI

Kenni Lowry Mystery Series

Mysteries so delicious it'll make your mouth water and leave you hankerin' for more.

FIXIN' TO DIE
SOUTHERN FRIED
AX TO GRIND
SIX FEET UNDER
DEAD AS A DOORNAIL
TANGLED UP IN TINSEL
DIGGIN' UP DIRT
BLOWIN' UP A MURDER
HEAVENS TO BRIBERY

Magical Cures Mystery Series

Welcome to Whispering Falls where magic and mystery collide.

A CHARMING CRIME
A CHARMING CURE

A CHARMING POTION (novella)
A CHARMING WISH
A CHARMING SPELL
A CHARMING MAGIC
A CHARMING SECRET
A CHARMING CHRISTMAS (novella)
A CHARMING FATALITY
A CHARMING DEATH (novella)
A CHARMING GHOST
A CHARMING HEX
A CHARMING VOODOO
A CHARMING CORPSE
A CHARMING MISFORTUNE
A CHARMING BLEND (CROSSOVER WITH A KILLER COFFEE COZY)
A CHARMING DECEPTION

Mail Carrier Cozy Mystery Series

Welcome to Sugar Creek Gap where more than the mail is being delivered.

STAMPED OUT
ADDRESS FOR MURDER
ALL SHE WROTE
RETURN TO SENDER
FIRST CLASS KILLER
POST MORTEM
DEADLY DELIVERY
RED LETTER SLAY

Maisie Doss Mystery

SLEIGHT OF HAND

About Tonya

Tonya has written over 100 novels, all of which have graced numerous bestseller lists, including the USA Today. *Best known for stories charged with emotion and humor and filled with flawed characters, her novels have garnered reader praise and glowing critical reviews. She lives with her husband and a very spoiled rescue cat named Ro. Tonya grew up in the small southern Kentucky town of Nicholasville. Now that her four boys are grown men, Tonya writes full-time in her camper she calls her SHAMPER (she-camper).*

Learn more about her be sure to check out her website tonyakappes.com. Find her on Facebook, Twitter, BookBub, and Instagram

Sign up to receive her newsletter, where you'll get free books, exclusive bonus content, and news of her releases and sales.

If you liked this book, please take a few minutes to leave a review now! Authors (Tonya included) really appreciate this, and it helps draw more readers to books they might like. Thanks!

Made in the USA
Monee, IL
16 June 2025